I
PROMISE
YOU

Susan Harris

To: Jane

Thank you for your Support

Susan Harr

Published in 2013 by FeedARead.com Publishing –
Arts Council funded

A CIP catalogue record for this title is available from
the British Library.

I would like to thank my mother for her continued support. She told me never to underestimate my abilities, and always try new things.

She has been an inspiration to me and my family and this is dedicated to you...

Acknowledgements

I would like to say a big thank you to my husband and the fact he couldn't wait to read my first book.

To my children AM and AL for allowing mommy to be anti-social.

To my family who gave me the love and support to keep going.

And to all my friends

Thank You All

Chapter One

Happy Birthday to me

I woke up with a big smile on my face. Not only was it my birthday but I had planned to go out with a bang.

As I lay on my bed, my mind started to wonder about Jack, my long term boyfriend of three years. I met Jack on a night out with my best friend Isabelle. She was drunk and was flirting with him, but for some reason he preferred me and I wouldn't swap that for the world.

He was planning a special evening for me, "would it be dinner and sex," sex then dinner or just sex, I chuckled to myself knowing that I would have to wait several long hours to find out, *what a bummer*.

Slipping out of bed, I took a long deserved shower to cool off my wondering mind, and get myself ready for work.

I slipped into my black lace bra and thong, my favourite black figure-hugging dress, stockings and high heels, keen for everyone to know that I was looking hot at twenty four.

I have curly black hair that swings just past my shoulders, my curves are all in the right places, I'm five feet, seven inches, sexy long legs, a petite waist and a chest to make any man dribble, "Yep" I love how I look and how it leaves men saying *"if only"* and yes, I do love myself if you haven't gathered that by now as I laugh and say to myself, *Autum Jones, you're a bad girl.*

The office was full today; there was Janice on reception, with the most amazing emerald green eyes that could easily put you in a trance, her blond bobbed hair, and her five feet nothing frame. She was wearing her blue blazer, matching skirt and a white blouse with the company's logo, this look was completed with a little scarf, making her look more like an air stewardess than a receptionist.

Then there's Bob our security guard, he's in his late thirties, around six feet tall with a medium athletic build, short black hair and sky blue eyes.

I say "hi" to them both as I make my way into the lift.

As I come out onto the fourth floor, Isabelle meets me half way down the office; she is my best friend and is always keen to fill me in on the daily gossip.

"Happy Birthday" she says, as she presents me with presents that I can clearly see hidden behind her back. I reply with a "thank you" as she starts to drag me to my desk. "What are your plans for tonight then, I know a great Italian not far from here, we can go for a meal if you like then go dancing"

"Sorry Isabelle but Jack is surprising me tonight and if it is what I think it is you may be seeing a lovely sparkler on my finger!"

"OMG, OMG he is never going to propose is he?"

"Don't sound so shocked it's been three years remember"

"I know it just seems so… come here" she says as she grabs me for a hug.

"Congratulations, I know he makes you happy.

"Thank You."

The morning flew by, and I was having such a lovely day opening up my presents that the office staff had bought me. Jack had sent me some long stem lilies via Interflora which are my favourite and a note which said "To my true love."

I just could not stop grinning to myself until my boss; Mr. Frank Lucas came over to me.

Frank was thirty years old, good looking, slim, and tanned. He was also well groomed and had the deepest sexy voice you have ever heard. "Happy Birthday Autum"

"Um thanks Mr. Lucas." I could feel myself blushing as his voice went straight through me and down to my spine making me blush even more, that voice got me every time.

Lunchtime came and went in a flash and I knew that soon I would be spending the evening with Jack.

At five o'clock, I danced my way out of the building with my presents and flowers, my mind fixed on the evening ahead and what Jack had planned for me. I arrived back at my apartment at five, forty five.

Jack had been sending me text messages all day but the last one said "wear something sexy, pick you up at eight" and that he loved me. "Ahh my man loves me has that special 'ring' to it, *hopefully my ring!!!*"

Snap out of it, I thought. I had just over two hours to get ready and I needed to look sexy and hot. Having washed and blow dried my hair, I picked a G String to match my red dress that I had bought just the week before; it was backless so there was no need to wear a bra. The less I had on, the quicker it would be to take off! Before I had even blinked the buzzer was going.

"Hi it's me, buzz me up."

My heart started to race at the thought of seeing Jack. We had been together for so long we just had this connection.

As I opened the door Jack just looked amazing, dressed in a black suit and tie; he looked edible.

"Wow, you look hot" I gasped.

"Don't look so bad yourself," we both laughed in unison.

As he came closer, my breath started to become shallow; he oozed sex appeal, with his dark brown shoulder length hair, my favourite aftershave and his five feet, nine inch frame heading my way, as he put his arms around my waist I knew that "sex" would come before dinner.

His lips met mine and I opened my mouth to except his tongue. As our bodies became entwined my hands pulled back his jacket until it dropped to the floor.

I loosened his tie and took it up over his head as he began to undo his shirt, nearly ripping it off in the process; he took in a breath to say "Happy Birthday."

He teased my dress from off my shoulders, as it fell slowly past my already hard nipples, down past my waist and on to the floor.

I could feel his erection pressing into me as he took off his trousers. I was already wet with desire and he was hard with lust as he pinned me to the wall. He slipped his hands on the side of my waist, and then slowly took off my G string, making me ache.

"Is this my present I gasped?"

"No, this is just an appetiser" he cried back.

His tongue eventually left my ever swelling pink lips and circled around my nipples. He started to suck hard, grabbing them both and trying to fit them into his mouth.

He was parting my legs with his knee.

God, this felt good I thought, using my free hands, I slid his boxers over his manhood pulling him closer, his erection bouncing into action and pressing into my stomach.

He inched a finger between my legs then gently glided it back and fourth against my clit; I wanted to come there and then I was so wet.

He then inserted one finger inside me, then another. "What do you want me to do?" he asked.

"I want more" I replied.

He inserted another finger as I opened my legs wider to accommodate.

I tightened my grip to make the sensation more intense. "I want you now" I said, as I wrapped my legs around his waist, putting my hands around his neck for support and arching my back into the wall, he held me in place, his hands on my ass.

He removed his fingers and guides his hard cock to my entrance before entering me.

I moaned with pleasure as his cock filled up my space, wanting more of my man. His breathing by my ear just made me quiver inside as I felt a gush of air from him.

"Fuck me" I shouted. "I want to feel every inch of you inside me"

As he lifted me slightly higher I could feel him penetrating me deeper.

"Keep going" I said as he rocked into me, barely catching my breath.

I could feel the build up getting stronger and stronger from both of us, with his breathing getting faster and me getting so close.

"Take me harder" I whispered as he pumped inside me. I knew I could no longer hold back as he gripped my ass tighter. I tilted my head back as I came, groaning at the same time. I could feel my insides tightening around him, sucking and urging him to come too.

His breathing was now very loud and his cock was so hard: I knew he was ready.

He cried out as I felt the warmth of him spilling inside me. His head flopped to my neck and I felt his breathing slowing, until it returning to normal as he kissed me.

He carried me towards the bed as we both curled up together, hot and sweaty from our love making.

"If that was my appetiser, I cannot wait for my main."

Jack laughed and grinned as he told me that would come a little later.

"We need to get a move on, it's already late and Margo's is booked for nine, thirty."

After a quick shower we both quickly dressed and went to eat.

Margo's was a lovely place but not cheap. It was draped in thick velvet wallpaper, with sweeping chandeliers and just the right type of music in the background, meaning that you could close your eyes and pretend you were somewhere exotic.

Jack had already pre-ordered for us both. My favourite "Bollinger" champagne was flowing, and we laughed and joked about the day I had at work and about how Mr. Lucas wished me a Happy Birthday.

"Talking about Birthdays, haven't you forgotten something" I said.

"I thought I was all you needed" he replied, with a sly grin.

I gave him an "I'm so in love with you smile" but deep down I hoped he was joking about my present.

As our starter came he had still not mentioned or produced anything for my birthday. The main came and still nothing, then desert. By that time Jack had started to make general conversation. I knew he was talking to me because I saw his lips move, and I knew I was smiling back at him but my mind had started to wander.

All I thought about was where my present may be. "Why is he taking so long to give it to me, and if he thinks he is getting anything when we get back to my apartment he has another thing coming!"

That was when I heard Jack calling my name.

"Are you ok? You seem to have drifted off there. Was everything ok with your meal?"

"Yes it was lovely thanks, all this excitement just got to me that's all." I mean how could I just say "where's my damn present"

Jack paid for the bill and we headed back to my apartment. It was now just before midnight and my birthday was coming to an end.

As we went inside, Jack said "did you really think I would forget your birthday?" My heart started to pound: he was teasing me all this time and it had worked.

A grin came to my face although it was more like a smile: a smile so big that all my teeth were showing as I clapped my hands. Yep, I was a child waiting to be given her present. I was just beaming with excitement.

He pulled something out of his jacket pocket that I had ripped off earlier, it was a box, but not just any box, this was a box which could possibly hold a ring, *my ring,*

If it was earrings, then he was going to learn the meaning of "not tonight, I have a headache" - a permanent one.

I clapped my hands together again like a silly little schoolgirl; *umm that's a nice idea must buy myself that outfit!*

He opened the box and there it was: my big, shiny, diamond-encrusted, heart-shaped white gold platinum ring.

My heart skipped a beat and I knew that this was the best present I could ever have wished for; the only one I wished for.

I was trying to hold back the tears but they started to flow.

"I love you" he said, "and I want you to be my wife, and if you say yes, I promise you that I'll make you the happiest women ever."

14

As he placed the ring on my finger, I was so overwhelmed I just stood there, frozen. I couldn't move or say anything.

It felt like an eternity.

"Well, what do you think?"

Looking up at him I said "I love it, and yes I cannot wait to be your wife too."

"There is only one other thing I ask of you", he said.

"Here we go, demands already, don't go out with the girls, get my dinner on the table, make sure you're naked when I come in from work, well the last one I can do."

"What is it??" I exclaimed.

"I want to see you naked, wearing that and your killer heels in bed tonight"

Now he's talking my language.

Before I knew it Jack was on the bed naked, his cock so hard and solid, much like the rock he had just given me.

I climbed on top of him and spread my legs apart; I licked his earlobes and planted a kiss there before using my tongue to find my prey. His lips were ripe and I was seduced to explore them further. The tip of my tongue circled the outline of his top lip before I let go, I repeated it again with his bottom lip as I prized open his mouth for access and plunged my tongue in before slowly pulling it out whilst picturing that this was his cock inside of my mouth, warm and moist.

I circled my tongue around the top of his nipples, flicking and biting them as I went.

"That's nice" he said as he relaxed deeper into the bed, I planted kisses all around them as I moved further down.

My tongue swirled around his chest as I felt him hardening below me.

I pinched his nipples with my fingers to increase the pleasure and he moaned, his cock rising in approval.

I moved down his waist and took his cock in my hand slowly moving it up and down. He tilted his head back and moaned even more, his body telling me to go on.

I released my hand and slid my body down again so that I could take him in my mouth.

The tip of his cock was starting to spill his seed and by now he was wet, and so was I; the thought excited me more as I circled the tip with my tongue before I pushed it all the way in.

He grabbed my head, placing his hands for support, he starting to gently guide me up and down, telling me how good it felt with his raspy sexual voice.

They were short strokes at first, as he moved his hips at the same time bringing himself up to meet me.

"I can't get enough of you" his voice broken and hoarse between his heavy breaths.

I could feel his erection getting harder, and his body movements changing.

In and out my mouth it went, deep in the back of my throat as far as it would go, I grabbed his balls in my hand and listened to the deep raspy groans that he was producing.

I pulled it out and licked around the tip before sliding it back using my teeth as I went, his veins were on the verge of popping.

I knew then, that he wanted release!

He grabbed the sheets with his hand as he said "yes, oh yes." I gripped him harder as I worked him, squeezing his balls all the time so his cock hardened even more in my mouth.

His head went back deeper into the bed, his body starting to shake intermittently as he filled me with his juices, he cried out, as he came again and again, before finally relaxing on the bed.

A few minutes later I was the one laying on the bed horny as hell.

Jack was in full swing and my fire was well and truly lit.

My nipples were like bullets waiting to be fired and as he licked, flicked and sucked them with the tip of his tongue, well what can I say, what a feeling. It travelled from my head all the way down between my legs adding to the sensation.

He works his way down with his tongue, and then back up again.

Always teasing, heightening the pleasure.

He cupped my breast in his mouth and sucked for dear life.

My legs already spread apart ready to welcome him into my fold, Jack teased my clit as he worked his tongue inside and out making me cry out with pleasure.

I gripped the sheet to steady myself.

"Deeper, just deeper" I told him, and upon hearing my wish he slid his manhood inside, thrusting so hard that my head was banging against the headboard before I knew it.

"Harder, harder" I told him, as I found myself unable to control my breathing. This was good, and this was how I liked to be fucked, not slow and sensual but fast and furious.

I call it my "Dirty Fuck."

I came so quick I nearly passed out from the pleasure, as I dug my nails into his ass and climaxed for a second time that night, my poor clit was begging for mercy and throbbing like a bad headache but what a birthday present I won't forget in a hurry.

Chapter Two

For all those ladies out there, why is it that when we get that sparkler, we seem to go around shoving it in someone's face.

As I arrived at work on Monday it was like my left hand belonged to an alien. As I glided past reception my left hand somehow found itself in Janice's face.

"Are you?"

"Yes" I said as I tried to stop smiling. As I went out onto the office floor Isabelle came running towards me screaming down the office.

"Is that what I think it is?"

"Yes it is."

"OMG, I want all the goss, what happened? Did he get down on one knee? Where did you go? How comes you never rang me last night?" She went on and on with the questions. By the time I filled in Isabelle with the gossip and how the sex was so amazing I thought she was about to come herself, I couldn't stop laughing.

As I reached my desk, there was a note asking me to see Mr. Lucas, *"great"*

His office was down the end of a long hallway, you had to go through two double doors before you came to his room and that is after going up seven more floors.

I would then have to wait for his PA to announce that I had arrived, before being ushered in like someone who has been told to see the head teacher and waiting impatiently for all to see that you have been bad girl!

Frank had worked his way up within the business and the rewards were plain to see. His office was hugh, boardroom table took up quite a space, including a large office desk in a semi-circle shape.

His leather high back chair was such a centre piece that you could not see him if his back was towards the window, his cabinets were full of books and different awards that I was unsure what they were for and his walls were decorated with pictures of black tie events, conferences and certificates all related to him and some of his associates; besides this he had no family pictures decorating his desk, which I found unusual.

"You wanted to see me Mr. Lucas?"

"Please call me Frank", *uncomfortable.*

"Oh sorry, Frank"

"Please sit"

I crossed my legs sitting down facing him but making sure that my ring was in full view.

Getting up from behind his desk he came around to the other side.

"Nice ring"

"Thank you, my fiancé gave it to me last night," *amongst other things as I smiled to myself.*

"Congratulations" he said in a thoughtful manner. "Anyway I know you may be wondering why I called you here. We have been given a great opportunity to see some of our top clients, at our head office in Miami some of whom you have already been dealing with."

Did he just say Miami, as in South Beach, Sun and Shopping?

"There will be four of us in total, and the reason I would like you to come is because you're very good at closing deals, one of my best, and I would like you on the team."

"Me? I would love to go shopping" I said quickly without thinking.

"I mean, I would love to go," *blushing as I tried to sound professional.*

Frank gave a chuckle.

"Who would be the others if you don't mind me asking?"

"There would be myself of course," *of course,* "Rebecca and Julian."

Julian was in his mid-twenties. He was Jamaican born but still had that twang of an accent about him when he got in full flow.

At six feet, two inches he liked to keep fit, and had a chest most men would die for, as well as a nice butt.

Well, it would be hard to miss him plus he was loved by everyone.

I was glad that Rebecca was coming as I didn't like the thought of possibly being the only girl going and having no one to shop with, I mean work with. I smile again to myself.

"When is this taking place?"

"A fortnight today, so make sure that you have a valid passport to hand," although he knew I did.

I have been on other trips before with different people in the office, Canada, Detroit, New York so I knew I had to always have my passport in tow. As I walked out of the office I saw Rebecca staring at me, she must have already known that I was going but she did not say a word, *I'll get her back for that.*

What was I going to tell Jack? Well to be honest this was just another trip; he should be used to it by now.

I found out from Rebecca that this trip was for two weeks. I just presumed it would only be a short trip. I had never been away for that long before. Four or five night's maybe, but never two weeks. "How can I cope without sex for that long?" *For goodness sake listen to myself, I sound like an addict.*

Two weeks passed by so quickly, and I could not believe that I was packing my suitcase, checking my passport and documents and getting ready to leave for the airport.

Jack wanted to see me off. We had a great night together and I was all sexed up and still in a great mood. I did not want to spoil it by getting teary at the airport, especially not in front of my colleagues.

I told Jack to keep an eye on my place for me as he also had a spare set of keys, although he would only use them if he knew that I was not there or I had told him to let himself in, *bless.*

It was still unusual to see Frank in casual clothing; sometimes I forgot that he was not my boss twenty four, seven.

He wore casual jeans and a white polo shirt.

Julian wore a T-Shirt which said "if you can't resist me kiss me" and a pair of jeans whilst Rebecca wore a summer dress just above the knee.

Well I also wore a summer dress, as I knew the weather would be nice, *ninety degrees nice* and did not want to arrive all sticky.

I had the window seat on the plane next to Frank, *great* and Rebecca got to sit next to Julian in the row behind us.

I watched the in-flight movies as I wasn't sure I could hold a conversation for that long without running out of things to say.

Half way through movie number two, I must have dosed off, and when I woke Frank was sleeping on my shoulder.

I tried not to be rude, so pretended to turn myself towards the window and then he made some deep sexy noise and faced the other way.

Rebecca and Julian were also asleep "together" *how comes I missed that*; they must have been keeping that one under raps.

"Great" I thought, so much for girlie chats together, she will probably end up spending most of her evenings with Julian but hey, nothing I can do about it, will speak to her when we arrive at our hotel and find out what the deal is between the two of them.

Going through customs was a breeze, we all got through without any hassle.

Why is it that you know you have nothing to hide, but you make yourself feel guilty going through security?

We collected all of our belongings and headed for a cab. You really feel the heat when you come out of the air conditioned airport and the heat hits you even harder when you go outside; it takes your breath away.

"Welcome to Miami"

The journey to the hotel took less than twenty five minutes. We were staying at a beach front hotel on South Beach and the sun was as hot as hell, *my kind of heaven.*

We checked in and Frank had booked us into separate rooms all on different floors. Mine was on the fourth floor number 219, and as I swiped my card and entered the room, I was blown away.

I had a view overlooking South Beach on the main stretch, a living room which had an L shaped tan leather sofa, a bed big enough to have a mini party in with a great walk in wardrobe, two wash basins and a Jacuzzi bath with power shower in the corner. There were also fancy lights glowing for any mood, it was just great. "Thanks Frank"

We were all meeting up at seven, thirty for dinner which gave us some time to chill in our rooms and just relax.

I phoned Jack to let him know that I had arrived and that my room was just the best. At dinner, Rebecca was describing her room, two times twin beds, and table and chairs etc. *not as nice as mine.*

Julian's was about the same only he had what sounded like a triple bed and a jacuzzi bath which he loved. *Watch out Rebecca.*

I was going to play down mine but I thought that they may see it if they popped up to visit me and I didn't want them to think that I was getting any special treatment; to me this was just another regular trip.

"Wow" Rebecca and Julian said in unison. "You must let us see it after dinner." I blushed a bit, why, I'm not sure, maybe because Frank was just listening to the conversation but not really saying anything and it just felt awkward.

To take the talk off myself I asked Frank what his room was like. He picked up his glass of JD & coke and just said "why don't you come up and see for yourself." *Smile it off, don't get embarrassed, you can do this*, nope, it didn't work. I was as red as the beetroot salad that the waiter had just placed in front of me, Rebecca and Julian were on the verge of dribbling, mouths open and tongues spilling out.

"We'll all pop up and see it won't we guys"

I gave them that 'help me out look.'

"Uh yeah no problem," as they both started to snigger.

After dinner we all sat around the bar sipping drinks. I had my favourite chill out drink, Martini Rosso with lemonade, while Rebecca had Baileys & ice and Julian had rum neat of course. Frank stuck to his JD & coke. The atmosphere was good, it was nice to just talk generally about anything and everything, and by ten, thirty we decided to all call it a night, but as we headed for the lifts Rebecca decided to remind us all, or should I say me, that we were all going to have a look at Frank's room, prompting Frank to pipe up and say *"the more the merrier"*

The lift stopped at the top floor *"penthouse"* of course and we were just amazed at how much floor space it commanded.

It was like looking around the rich and famous houses but this was just one big floor space with plenty of doors leading off the main entrance to the lift.

"How many other guests occupy this floor" Julian asked, "only me" he replied.

I was so caught up in the moment that I did not see them going inside until they called me.

As I walked slowly into the room it was like being at the top of the CN Tower, just never ending 360 degree views all around you.

The night lights were shining through the windows as the world went by, and the room was filled with sofa upon sofa. The drinks cabinet was filled to the brim with booze, and there was a television big enough to make you think you were at the pictures; this room just went on and on.

"Wow, can we take a look around?"

"Help yourself"

"This must have cost a bomb" said Rebecca.

"I am entitled to some perks you know. I like my creature comforts when I'm away from home"

"Well there's perks and there's perks" I thought to myself.

We all headed to the left of the room where there was a fully fitted larger than normal white kitchen, complete with an american fridge, fresh fruit on display and plenty of wine. This was a kitchen you would use to entertain guests or have a business lunch with and a chef to cater for all your needs, what a life. Back through the door we came from, we headed through to the living room, and into another side room which lead to the bedrooms.

I say bedrooms as there were three in total, all en suite of course. There was also a walk in wardrobe you would die for and a bed big enough to house King Henry VIII. The top of this most gorgeous scenery led onto a roof terrace, we were just lost for words.

I started drifting off again in my thoughts, thinking

"What could I be doing in that big seductive bed while I wait for Jack to fuck me like mad?"

I felt myself getting a little flushed and a bit excited, my heart started to beat quick.

My breathing was getting fast as I felt a warm breath sweep past my ear; Rebecca was trying to tell me to stop daydreaming, so I pulled myself together and promised myself that when we left this mansion, or should I say "penthouse" I would call Jack.

Chapter Three

Why is it when we think of good times we want to be near the ones we love!

When I returned back to my room after being in Frank's, it seemed as if I was in a bedsit.

Everything looked so small for a while until my mind adjusted back to the space I knew it to be.

Sitting on the bed I phoned Jack, with the time difference he should have finished work by now and should be at home or at mine.

The phone did not even ring long before it asked me to leave a message after the tone. I was so disappointed that I had not been able to speak to Jack; all that excitement just faded when I heard the message,

I threw the phone on the bed and jumped in the shower, *where was he?*

Jack knew I would be ringing him roughly at this time.

Could he be caught up at work, stuck in traffic or was he off enjoying himself without me? Before I knew it doubt had taken over my mind, convincing me he was up to no good, even though I knew that was just not his style.

But still, it was there, lingering in the back of my mind like those images that you see just before you are due to eat your dinner, of all those starving children around the world as you're tucking into you're food, making you feel guilty for no reason.

When I came out of the shower my hair was wet and I had no interest in wrapping it up.

Every time I walked, water droplets would go all over the floor.

I patted myself dry before taking out those dolly type dryers that they leave in your room. I tried my best to bring life back to this wild, half curly, not so sure what to do with type of hair, when my phone started to ring.

Diving onto the bed, my towel decided to leap out of the way and flop to the floor to take cover.

"Hello Jack, is that you?"

"Of course it is who else would it be?"

That was all I needed to hear, the sound of his voice sweeping through me, making me all warm and ready to cuddle up with my pillow.

"Sorry I missed your call, went to the gym for an hour after work; need to look good for you when you come back home."

I started to laugh and rolled over onto my back. I was telling him about the day I had and how we all went into Frank's room and how big it was and the size of his bed.

Jack said "I'm getting jealous here."

"So am I, I want you here with me, in my bed I miss you Jack, miss you touching me, miss us making love, having cuddles, I just miss you."

"I miss you too," but it's only been a few hours. So! Are you in bed yet?"

"No, not yet just came out the shower."

"Are you *naked* then?" Jack said in that naughty tone of voice.

Looking down at myself I realised that the towel did actually abandoned ship and that I was indeed naked.

The only person missing in this picture was Jack, but not for very long.

I needed to think outside the box.

"Well, I think we need to try phone sex don't you?"

Jack laughed; "where did that come from?"

I told him that I needed to de-stress and what better way than by having a bit of phone sex. Something I had never tried before.

Jack had told me that he was sitting in his chair at home, and that he was wearing his favourite white addidas tracksuit with a sleeveless t-shirt underneath, and that he had already kicked off his trainers and his socks.

I told him to relax and close his eyes and picture me standing in front of him and that's how it began.

I'm bending slightly down to kiss his temples one by one then start to slide my tongue up and down his face.

My lips start to move kissing his cheeks, left then right, heading towards his mouth.

"Open your mouth" I whispered down the phone, "but not too wide, just enough for me to part them with my tongue but I want you to put up a little resistance."

"I'm going to go deep Jack, then deeper still.

Can you feel me?" As I listened into the phone I could hear Jack's breathing, shallow and quick. I felt that I had teleported myself into his room and could see everything and feel everything that I was doing to him.

I take off his tracksuit top, then his sleeveless t-shirt follows next, as a slowly pull it over his head to be flung over my shoulder, landing somewhere in his room.

I put my hands through his gorgeous hair to better my grip, my tongue leaving his mouth and moving towards his chest. I kneel between his legs slightly and see his chest slowly rising, up and down like he's in a yoga class going through the relaxation part before the class finishes and you're left totally revitalised but half asleep.

"Keep your eyes closed" I reminded him.

"I will, I promise" he replied in this soft, hypnotic voice.

As I adjust myself again so that my tongue circles his left nipple, I bite the thin hairs around them before I suck them in.

I hear him moan, and feel his manhood starting to wake and take notice.

I do the same on his right nipple as I feel his manhood pressing into my chest telling me that I now have his undivided attention.

I bend down on my knees and with my hands I tell him to slightly lift up so that I can remove his tracksuit bottom.

He tells me he is "commando" and I smile his erection starring at me like a stand off, warning me that it is not going down without a fight.

Believe me, I had no intention of it doing that either.

I told Jack to picture my hand around his cock, and to put his hand on top of mine then to move it up and down "slowly," and he does. Now picture it in my mouth.

Feel the warmness inside as you move it up and down, in and out but not too fast Jack, I want you to savour the moment.

I want you to keep this going for as long as possible, and tell me how it feels.

"So good, so good" and I smile to myself.

I told Jack that I am now taking it out of my mouth so that I can lick the tip with my tongue.

"Rub it with your finger Jack feel it, that's my tongue Jack circling you and it feels good, now put it back in my mouth again, that's it, now deeper.

I can feel it now Jack, at the back of my throat, getting bigger, stronger, and harder" Jack's breathing was getting even faster now, I knew he was about to come.

"I can't hold it much longer" he said.

"Feel me sucking you Jack, I want you to fuck me harder in my mouth; I want you to come, and come now"

He let out a moan; a moan that I was sure could be heard by his neighbours, his breathing was still quick and erratic and you could tell his body was shaking by the noises he was making.

It took some time for his breathing to get back to normal then I asked him if he was ok.

This was my first experience of phone sex and to be honest I thought I did pretty well.

"How was it?"

"Wow, babe what the hell was that? You sure there's nothing you need to tell me? That was amazing."

"How comes we've never done that before. I'm shocked we've never thought of doing this all the other times you have been away"

"Didn't realise what I would be missing" he laughed.

"Glad you liked it"

"Well, now I can breathe again, I think it's time I returned the favour"

I lie on my back with the biggest smile on my face, *bring it on!*

I started to relax and just let Jack's voice go through my body.

"I want your eyes open all the time"

I want you to feel me touching you, tasting you, and licking you, understand?"

"Understand," I said, a bit too excitedly.

"Now put the phone to your ear as close as you can get it, then take your hands and cup your breasts and squeeze them for me"

"Lick your index finger and play with your nipples, circle and pinch them until I tell you to stop, now lick your nipples with the tip of your tongue I know you can reach them"

"Tell me how that feels"

"It feels good, real good" I said with my already choppy breath.

"Bring your knees slightly up towards you and move you're hands down, towards your navel, then to your thighs and part your legs slowly for me"

I could feel myself getting aroused, my nipples getting hard, and my skin starting to prickle.

This was good, better than good and I was hoping it was going to get a whole lot better.

"I want you to put your finger in your mouth again and suck it"

"Suck it the same way you suck my cock. I smiled, if I do it the same way, I could see myself getting jaw ache.

"Keep going fast then slow, fast then slow". I started to moan as I closed my eyes for a second.

"Now put a second finger in until it's nice and wet, open your legs wider and take your index finger and stroke your pussy". *Oh god, this was good.*

I heard a noise and wandered where it was coming from, until I realised it was me, my moans of pleasure louder than I expected them to be. I was feeling a bit embarrassed that this was me, naked on my bed having phone sex, but this embarrassment didn't last long.

Jack was fucking me down the phone.

Should I be enjoying this? Hell yes!!

"Keep going but faster, now put your fingers inside and go as deep as you can.

Before I knew it, I had raised my hips off the bed and was working myself with my fingers in harmony with the fluid movements of my body. As my hips went up, my fingers were going down, deep into my body and taking over my mind.

I was getting lost in this world of self pleasure; my left hand was playing with my breast, stroking and pinching the tips of my nipples. All I knew was that every part of my body was going to getting a full workout.

I spread my legs even further apart, as the feeling was becoming more intense.

If Jack was speaking to me then my mind had gone blank. In and out my fingers went, wetter and wetter every time.

My heart felt like it was about to give up. I could feel it, feel the sensation building and building. As I took hold of the sheets to brace myself, I let out a scream, a scream like no other, my body shaking and trembling with the force of my orgasm.

I hoped that the hotel staff would not burst in and see what caused me to make this undignified noise with my fingers still inside me being sucked and sucked by some invisible force.

"Autum, Autum are you ok? I thought I'd lost you for a moment"

Still breathless and wet with my legs now flopping outwards and my insides still throbbing I replied "I'm fine honey, just didn't realise how good that could be"

"Well, promise not to replace me with that finger will you"

"I won't" I said, as we both laughed.

Before I knew it we were into our second week of our working holiday. Frank went jogging most mornings before work, along with Julian his new buddy and in a way I was glad.

Rebecca and I had managed to have some girlie time together when we went out shopping.

"So how serious is it with you and Julian?"

"Oh just having a bit of fun, he is so charming and sweet and is such a great lover I can understand why he is a lady's man, he's hung like a.."

"Hold up girl, way too much information," and we both laughed.

"Julian says that Frank has been trying to find out some inside gossip on you and Jack"

"What? Why?"

"Not sure"

"What's he been asking about me?"

"Things like where you both met, does he often stay over, what do your friends think about him, and do they think he's good enough for you, things like that"

"What the hell! What if he stays over? What the fuck has that got to do with him?"

"Has he not said anything or hinted those things when you've been at dinner or at the bar at anytime since our stay even as a joke?"

"Never, why would he?"

"Maybe he finds you more attractive now you're engaged, men sometimes like the challenge"

I laughed it off as a seriously bad joke, but I was feeling uncomfortable and even more so, fucking pissed off!

Chapter Four

*Why do we always think that everyone is watching
and following us when we feel scared?
And is it a good sign to go in guns blazing.*

After returning from shopping with Rebecca I put my bags down and pondered over what she had said about Frank.

The more I thought about it, the more I was working myself up, and the more I worked myself up the more pissed off I got, so I decided there was only thing for it, *confrontation.*

I never thought of myself as the argumentative type, but I would pull no punches with Frank. He knew me well enough to know that I would speak as I find; this had stood me in good stead with the line of work I was in.

It would be like dealing with the men in the boardroom who think that I am just a clueless girl who knows nothing about business.

When it came to handling myself in business, by the time I'd finish with them they always remembered my face and my name rather than just my gorgeous ass.

"I can do this, yes I can"

"Do I want to do this? Not really, but I need answers so that I can put this stupid situation behind me"

"Has my temper calmed down? No"

Instead, it had moved up a notch as I slammed my hotel door and headed for Frank's suite.

In the elevator I looked at myself in the glass mirror, I looked like someone possessed.

Gone was the lovely smart looking loved up girl of last night and in her place was a she devil.

"Breathe" I told myself as my heart started pounding and my breathing did the same.

I heard the ping of the elevator, it was showtime.

As I knocked on the door and waited, I realised that I could do this the rational way and smile as best as I could, or the not so rational way and go in there all guns blazing.

Frank answered the door with a smile, and at that moment I knew which way this would be heading.

I pushed the door open just missing his smiley face and barged my way into his room.

I saw his lip trying to move, trying to say something, but the she devil took possession of my mouth and I let it all out.

"How dare you ask questions about me?"

"What gives you the fucking right to speak to Julian behind my back?"

"If you want to know anything about me and Jack then come right out and fucking ask me"

His mouth opened again to say something but I cut him off.

"What business is it of yours if Jack sleeps over? None, that's right; you have no right prying into my private life Frank, none at all"

As I tried to breathe I noticed that Frank was moving slowly towards me.

He was looking me straight in the eye at all times, every time he took one step he would stop, then repeating the process all over again.

Is he trying to intimidate me? I think so"

"Is it working? I'm about to find out"

Now that I cleared the air and could think about what I had just done, I realised that maybe I went a bit overboard. "Oh shit what have I done?" but I didn't care, I still needed answers.

"Answer me Frank, why?"

"You want to know why"? Because I fancy you.

"What?"

"You heard. I have fancied you since you first started to work for me and still fancy you now"

I wanted to see if your relationship with Jack was solid and strong and not just a passing phase in your life.

"You fancy me? But you've never ever given any indication that you liked me that way"

"Ever the professional, that's me. I know the age difference could have been a factor"

"God Frank you're not much older than me" *oh no, have I given him an indication that I don't mind him liking me?*

Frank continued to get closer!

"Well so there's no more misunderstandings, I will say the words slowly. Jack, and, I, are fine, happy, in love and plan to get married once we have set a date."

He was getting closer still, what should I do? He was now in front of me.

I backed up a little so that Frank was not in my face.

My breathing started to feel *"different"*

It should have been heavy and angry, but it felt *"ready and inviting"*

I started to go around Frank so that I could leave but he grabbed me by the waist and swung me around; before I knew it, he was kissing me.

I put my hand across his chest to fight him off, but his tongue was sliding in, twirling around, finding a home in my mouth as if it should have always been there.

I struggled with my mind as to why my grip on his chest seemed to be loosening and turning into more of a hug.

Why my hands were now sliding through his hair, trying to get a better grip instead of fighting him off? I didn't want to let him go.

My mouth was no longer fighting him, but welcoming his tongue more and more.

I could taste him; he had recently had strawberries and champagne, my favourite mix.

Now my mouth wanted to suck in all that flavour.

My breathing! *What the hell was going on with my breathing?*

He came up for air and looked at me, *shocked I think,* to which I felt the same.

As I took in some air myself, reality kicked in. What the hell was I doing? Like a bolt of lightning up my ass I jerked away, shocked, shamed and embarrassed about what I had just done and allowed to be done to me in return. I took a good look at myself, my clothes slightly roughed up from the friction of both our bodies together, and my breathing, *"how did I get this sexual breathing"*

Frank was still looking at me and I at him. I then glanced down to find that he had gotten *aroused* by me, and just like that I ran out of room.

I pressed the elevator button so many times my finger ached, and then prayed that he would not follow me out. I asked myself why did I do it. But most of all *why did I like it?"*

Frank looked on as Autum left his room; he remembered the look of shock on her face before she ran out and what had occurred only a few minutes ago.

He remembered her shouting at him, her face all flushed and angry, but all he wanted to do was to go to her, to try and calm her down. Her breathing was heavy and loud, but he just wanted to calm her down, he told himself.

Whilst she was leaving his room he had held out his hand to stop her and to explain, but then kissed her. *Why?* He didn't know.

As she was shouting at him his mind had drifted to her lips. They were pink and sexy and his body was being drawn to them.

He had tried to fight the urge but couldn't help himself.

Once his lips met hers he noticed they were so warm, soft and moist, his tongue slid inside her mouth so easily. *But how did it get in there?*

Chocolate & Mint, that's what he could taste in her mouth. She must have had an ice-cream while she was out. Her hands were on my chest trying to keep me from her, but then she moved her hands into my hair willingly and her mouth*, she opened it.*

Why? She wanted my tongue inside her?

Yes that's right; she invited me in, but why?

He could feel the connection between them. It was real, it was instant, and he thinks she knew it to.

She must have felt it too before she pulled away, probably shocked at what she found herself doing, did she notice when she looked down at herself and at me how she had made me get *aroused?* He thought she did.

I ran back to my room and stripped off my clothes and took a shower, scrubbing myself clean as if I had tripped over and fallen in a pile of shit, as shit is how I was feeling right now.

I cried to myself as I didn't know what else to do and replayed what had just happened.

Went to Frank's room pissed as hell (check)

Felt empowered (check) breathing heavy, started to kiss, enjoyed kiss, wanted more, ok, no need to replay, just needed to know how I was going to deal with this.

I didn't fancy him, *did I?* Had I ever fancied him? Not that I knew of.

So what happened up there?

Did my subconscious like the fact that he fancied me?

Was I slightly turned on by that? I must have been, oh god, what had I done?

After my shower I laid on my bed and without realising I drifted off to sleep.

I could hear a phone ringing but thought I was still dreaming until I jumped out of bed.

It was now seven in the evening, time for dinner.

The phone was still ringing when I decided that I needed to answer it as I did not want anyone to come up to my room.

"Hello"

"Wow Autum did I wake you?"

Thank goodness it was Rebecca.

"Just dosed off for a bit you know, all that sun and shopping must have taken it right out of me"

"Are you coming down for dinner as I was just about to order some drinks"

"No, not tonight may just order room service as I still feel tired"

"You as well" says Rebecca.

"What do you mean?"

"Frank has also cried off, nothing going on that I should know about is there?"

"Don't be so fucking stupid Rebecca you know I'm engaged, why should there be anything going on between me and Frank?"

"Jesus, I was only joking Autum what's got into you?"

Talk about hanging myself.

"Sorry, just tired"

"Do you want any company?"

"No thanks, I might come down after all, just give me five minutes."

I arrived for dinner, and in a way was glad, as I was famished. We talked about our shopping trip to Julian and mentioned some of the items we bought as well as the fabulous ice-cream parlour we found which served the most awesome flavoured ice-creams known to man.

I explained that I had chocolate and mint and Rebecca had pecan.

"So, Rebecca tells me that Frank had been asking some questions about my private life?"

Julian looked at Rebecca as if to say "big mouth"

"Don't worry its fine"

"I'm just curious why he wanted to know," *like I don't already.*

"Well to be honest he was really embarrassed about asking. He was a little shy, and kept blushing, then kept telling me just to forget that he had asked the questions in the first place."

Frank shy, embarrassed, no way, I never would have thought he was that type of guy!

"Oh, there was one thing that I found out though"

"What's that?"

"I think he has a crush on you, a man thing you know, you ladies wouldn't understand"

Rebecca and I both started to laugh.

As the night was drawing on, I was still hungry but did not have the stomach for food even though my belly was telling me otherwise so I ordered light.

I started to feel guilty about the way I had over reacted when I went to see him.

I also realised that I could not just blame him as I also *willingly* contributed.

I needed to sort this out before tomorrow but was unsure as to how.

It was now ten o'clock. when I went back to my room and I decided to ring Frank and ask him to meet me downstairs.

On dialling his room my heart was pounding as I tried to think of things that I was going to say, but when I heard a quiet "hello" I knew then that Frank must be feeling just as bad as I did.

"Hi Frank it's me"

The line was quiet, nothing! All I could hear was the sound of his breathing.

"I think we need to talk about what happened this afternoon and I wandered if we could meet downstairs in five minutes?"

Another silence, then "yes that's fine, I'll see you then" he said before hanging up.

I put the receiver down and got ready to meet Frank as I nervously made my way out of my room.

Frank was already by the lounge as I exited the elevator.

He was looking around and twisting his hands in-between each other. He looked agitated and nervous; did I do this to him?

He spotted me and gave me a smile which took ages to reach its full meaning; I smiled back and approached the lounge.

We stared around for what seemed like ages, me looking up and down and Frank doing the same but at opposite times so we never seemed to be looking at each other. We needed to break the ice, and I was about to say something when Frank spoke.

"I'm so sorry Autum, can you forgive me? I didn't mean to hurt or upset you earlier I just, well I just"

"It's ok Frank, I'm not sure myself what happened up there but we both did things that we shouldn't have, I think we just need to move on and put it behind us don't you?" Frank looked up at me and there it was that pain in my chest and my stomach starts to tingle, *how did he do that?*

I looked away sharply as I felt myself blushing.

"Are you sure you're ok?"

"I'm fine"

I wanted to lighten the mood so I asked him if he had anything to eat, to which he replied "no." I called a waiter over and asked if we were too late to order food, with a shake of his head he said no.

Frank looked at the bar menu and ordered steak (medium rare) with mixed salad and vegetables.

I reminded Frank that we had a busy day ahead of us tomorrow and we would need our wits about us if we were to close this deal.

I also reminded him that we were a damm good team, and that I could not do this without him.

He relaxed his shoulders a little and let out a deep sigh as he repeated the words "so sorry" under his breath.

It was then I guess that I realised how upset Frank was about what took place earlier. This was a man who I had known for years, but it took minutes to reduce him to this.

We've had laughs, drinks after work now and then and both of us have had our fair shares of moans about life but now, I feel that I don't know this lost soul in front of me. I never thought he had a sensitive side, a caring for others before himself side until now, *and I liked it.*

I watched him properly for the first time as he ate his meal, the way he tenderly held his steak knife and how he sometimes slides his index finger up and down the handle.

How he cuts his steak pieces in a certain way always to the left, the way he scoops his vegetables over the steak before placing them carefully into his mouth.

How his tongue wraps itself around the food before he draws out the fork, and how he seemed to chew roughly the same amount of time before he swallowed, and how he always ate his salad first.

I stared at him eating, my mouth started to water, my belly started to rumble.

He looked up at me, paused for a few seconds, then slid the plate over to my side and told me to eat.

By this time my face was on fire with shame. How bad did I look and how loud was that rumble?

Why did I not just order something extra myself. I said "thank you" as I scooped the steak up and piled it in my mouth along with some vegetables.

I heard Frank laugh and I let myself smile. *We can work through this I told myself, tomorrow is another day.*

At just gone midnight we made our way back to the elevator. It had been a long day and I was tired. We both entered the lift and pressed our respective floor numbers.

I took a quick glance at Frank and he must have sensed it as he then looked at me and I just smiled.

The elevator announced my floor and I said goodnight to Frank before exiting.

As I turned around he said goodnight back and gave me a smile as the doors closed.

I got back to my room, undressed, brushed my teeth and curled up in my bed with my PJ's on before drifting straight off to sleep and to my dreams.

I'm in a playful mood; I see me and my friends at home having a sleepover.

There's me, Isabelle, Emily and Dionne. The music is loud and we have just watched our all time favourite film "the devil wears Prada"

There's popcorn all over my sofa, so we all move to the floor as the drinks start to flow.

We have JD, bailey's, vodka, rum and cider as we plan on getting totally wasted.

Dionne finishes her bottle of cider and wants to play the old classic game of "spin the bottle"

We giggle our way into a circle and I take the first spin, it lands on Emily, and I ask her "truth or dare" she goes for truth.

Isabelle asks her how many men she's had at one time.

I've known Emily since school and we have always been friends since. I think we all go through life with around a handful of genuine friends that you'll have for life and she was one of them.

She laughs and tells us that when she was at a freshman's ball that she was so drunk, she went back with two guys that she'd met that night. One was fucking her, as she takes the other in the mouth.

Once they had all "come" she swapped positions and repeated it all over again. She says she remembers having sex, but couldn't explain why her ass was hurting when she tried to sit down the next day, she starts to laugh as she recollects the event.

We all look at Emily and then at each other. This was the quiet girl in the class, the one who always stuck to her books and was hardly allowed outside of her home after school, boy! How things have changed.

Emily casually spins the bottle and it lands on Isabelle.

Isabelle goes for "dare"

We tell her to strip off to just her bra and thong and pretend she has been locked out of my flat and that she needs to use the phone so that we can let her in as the music is too loud but the phone is on the table and can easily be heard.

We all laugh.

Isabelle doesn't hesitate to strip off her PJ's. She has a figure to rival mine. She does have smaller breasts but they fit her frame nicely.

She knows some of my neighbours so she goes straight to Danny's which is right opposite my door.

Before knocking she turns back to see us laughing as we shut the door and all try to look through the peep hole as Danny answers the door.

His face is a picture; he looks shocked at first, and then tries his best not to look her up and down before letting her into his room.

I here my phone ring and Isabelle tells me to let her in.

We all run to open the door as she comes back in. Danny is still staring at her ass as I tell him thanks before we shut the door and roll about laughing; she is so brave I just love her.

She then slips back into her PJ's and the games continue.

I feel myself smiling in my sleep as my dream shifts onto a different scene. *I am now alone on a tropical beach somewhere.*

I have a room overlooking the pool and the beach. I like this dream.

The tropical trees around me have coconuts. I have a bikini on, white and gold in colour, and my hair is wet and I have a nice golden tan.

There's a cocktail in my hand and I go to sip it. I am unsure of what it is except that it's cold and nice.

As I take a stroll I see another house and head towards it.

There's laughter and giggles and I think to myself what a lovely sound.

When I get nearer, the sound I thought I heard turns out not to be laughter or giggles but the sound of moans and ooh's and ahh's, (god, they are having sex).

Instead of turning away I go closer, like some peeping tom.

Stepping towards the side of the house I look through the wooden slats and realised I am right, they sure are having sex.

His back is facing me and she is on the bed on all fours.

The bed is rocking with the force of his thrusts, and they carry on moaning loud as he grips onto her waist and ploughs deeper and deeper inside her. She is calling out for him to fuck her hard, with sweat running down his back as he continues.

"I love you" he says as he adjusts his grip on her.

"I love you too" she says as she tells him she is about to come and gives out a scream as she climax's. He follows soon after, collapsing on top of her, they then both turn over and lay face up on the bed.

It is only then, as I look at them that I realised that I knew these two people, it was me, and Frank.

Chapter Five

Why do we dream the way we dream? Are we missing something in our lives or is there a hidden message behind it.

I jolt up in my bed, sweating and panting. *"What the fuck"*

I checked the time and it was three, eighteen in the morning, I got out of bed and washed off my face. When I went to go to the toilet, I noticed that I was "moist" *please don't tell me that I got turned on by me and Frank?*

I felt distraught, disgusted and nauseous, that my subconscious was still playing around with my mind *"without my consent"*

I thought I had got over the incident yesterday, so why would I think of him in that way? I don't want him do I?

"But you asked him to fuck you hard"

"That was just a bad dream, when I get back to Jack this nonsense will stop and my life will get back to normal"

If you say so, but if that's the case then why were you enjoying yourself like that?

Not thinking about it, "get lost mind" and let me sleep "without having sex with my boss thank you."

I go back to my bed, dreading the night ahead of me, wandering if I would ever get some sleep. The next thing I heard was my wake up call from the hotel telling me it was six, forty five in the morning, *great!*

After a quick shower to wake myself up from my dreadful night I took a good look at myself and saw bags under my eyes and a sleepy face, *that's all I need.*

I wore my favourite close the deal red dress, a little cleavage showing at the front with its v neck shape, fitted waist and a small split at the back.

My hair was up and I left a few strands trickling down the side of my face.

I took out my killer red open toe shoes and put my jacket on before applying my red lipstick to finish off my look. I then headed for breakfast.

I joined up with the gang and they take one look at me and gasped.

For a split second I thought I had some toothpaste around my mouth or my lipstick had smudged onto my teeth, until they said how lovely I looked and that this deal would be signed, sealed and delivered within the next few hours.

I smiled and told them to stop kidding around and that I had worn this dress before.

I looked up at Frank who was still staring, although he quickly commented on how nice I looked.

We took our places for breakfast and went through the events of the day ahead.

This was our last day before heading home tomorrow and I realised that I had not spoken to Jack for the last two days. But what was worse, was that Jack had not tried to contact me either, *why?*

We left the hotel and arrived at our destination just before ten, thirty. On checking in we were told that the meeting had been cancelled and that they had tried to call Frank before he left the hotel but had missed him.

They could not re-schedule before we left but said that they would arrange a video conference when we got back to the UK and apologised again. Frank did not look pleased but he knew his hands were tied.

He called us all together and asked us what we wanted to do. He said that we could try for an earlier flight, do some shopping, top up our tans or whatever, he would go with the majority.

Rebecca and I were all shopped out so there was nothing more that I needed to buy as I had bought all my presents for everyone throughout our stay.

Julian was not a shopper and was happy to just chill. Frank was the only one left to reply.

He had decided that once we got back to the hotel, he would make some calls and see if there was any availability for us to catch an earlier flight. Rebecca and I clapped our hands. *I will see Jack earlier than I thought what a great surprise, especially if he is still at my flat, but best of all, is that by tomorrow I go back to normality.*

Frank was the best. He got us an earlier flight which was kind of him, and we had to check in three hours early so had plenty of time before our flight at six o'clock.

Most of my stuff was packed as I like to prepare for my journey home a few days before. I did not have many more things to put in except my toiletries.

I changed my clothes into something more comfortable for the long flight home; just some jeans a top and some open toed sandals.

We met back in the reception and called a cab.

Check in was quick and efficient so we just spent some time looking around duty free, *we all know you can never have enough perfume and booze.*

I bought some sprits and my all time favourite perfume, Chanel Number five. I then headed towards the checkout.

On the plane, Frank sat beside me.

I did not mind as we had sorted things out and I felt more comfortable around him again.

In a way it was just like old times. We chatted about future projects and that he was thinking of taking some time out when we got back, to go to his lodge in Lincolnshire, right on the golf course.

He would get his PA to re-arrange things whilst he was out.

It was nice listening to Frank, but I could honestly say he needed the break. He was looking tired *and who caused that?*

And a break from seeing me might do him the world of good, *but would it do me?*

He asked if I had plans when I got back home, but I just said it would be nice to spend some quality time with Jack before work on Monday.

Frank smiled and replied, "You deserve the quality time and thanks again for all your help"

"It's my job and thanks again for this opportunity"

I settled in for the movie but as I did not sleep very well the night before I just wanted to rest. *Too busy getting wet for your boss that's why!*

I shook that idea from my head and quickly nodded off into a deep sleep.

Frank woke me when the food trolley was coming and I ordered myself a bottle of white wine to go with dinner.

Rebecca and Julian were happily laughing and joking in front of us and turned around on occasions for the odd chat.

It was weird in a way as back in the office we all got on but this trip with us all had just bought us that bit closer.

I knew that if I had to work alongside these guys again I would do it in a heartbeat. I looked at my watch and knew that we had around two hours left before we landed.

My heart fluttered as I thought about it, as if nervous.

I was happy to be going home but anxious in a way, I just couldn't fathom out why.

The rest of the flight went by quick and soon we were being told to fasten our seatbelts for landing.

On the journey back home we all jumped into the same cab as Frank insisted on paying for us all, *which means he will of course claim it back.*

Rebecca was the first drop off; she lived in a newly built apartment block around ten minutes from work and from my block.

We said our goodbyes and see you on Monday speeches.

Julian was next. I did not realise he lived so close to both myself and Rebecca's apartment around another five minute drive.

Then it was my turn, a few minutes later and I was home.

I thanked Frank again for the lift and wished him a nice break, got my luggage, waved him goodbye and headed for my apartment, *home sweet home.*

It was eleven at night by the time I headed into the block, excited but tired. I knew that even though I wanted to see Jack, I hoped he wasn't there as I needed a good night's sleep.

As I approached my door I was conscious of how late it was and quietly slipped my keys in before entering.

I dropped my luggage by the front entrance and realised that Jack had left the telly on. He was here and deep down that made me happy.

It was quite loud and sounded as if it was coming from my bedroom which meant he had been staying here, but as I got closer I knew that something was wrong with this scenario. Yes I heard noises and yes it was coming from my bedroom but I also knew that I didn't have a telly in my room.

The bedroom door was slightly ajar so I could look through with ease.

I saw Jack naked and for a split second I nearly burst into the room ready to join him, jet lag forgotten.

His back was towards me and that was when I noticed that someone else's legs were wrapped over his shoulders.

I could hear Jack panting, moaning and sweating but my brain just couldn't process what was happening.

Jack was on top of some woman, in my apartment and in my bed.

He was god damn fucking some bitch in my bed *while I have been fucking slogging my god damn ass off with work.*

How could he bring some whore into my house?

I always thought that Jack and I could fuck, but he was fucking her like crazy, even the speed at which they were going was off the hook.

This bitch started to tell Jack to talk dirty to her and he did this with ease *as if he knew what she liked?*

"I'm going to fuck you so hard bitch, you won't close your legs for a week"

"More Jack," she said. "I'm going to pump so much shit in you, you're gonna leak for a month, then when I'm done with your pussy you're gonna suck my cock so hard in that big mouth of yours, you'll have your own meaning on how to suck a cuban cigar"

He then grabbed her around her hips and started to fuck her even harder causing *my* bed to squeak. I could hear the headboard bang, bang, banging with every thrust that he made.

"Yes" she cried. "That's it Jack, I'm coming. Don't stop" she said between panting breaths.

"Your pussy's so wet for me baby" he said.

"And your dick feels so sweet inside me" she replied. "I'm coming Jack, don't stop." Jack was panting like mad; sweat dripping off his back, his breathing out of control.

"Harder, yes like that, oh yes, yes" she cried as her head dropped back and she screamed out for dear life.

Now I know what you're thinking. I should have dragged that bitch out of my bed naked by her hair kicking and screaming, then thrown the bitch out of my apartment like the gutter rat she is, and yes that would have been good. No, it would have been great.

And as for that two timing wanker, well hoping that she gives him some disease that rots his dick off would also appease me, but at that moment in time I couldn't breathe properly, my vision was going blurred and I felt like I was going to be sick.

Just when I thought it couldn't get any worse, he says "that's it Isabelle, give it all to daddy" before exploding inside her and then collapsing on my bed.

Isabelle, no way, not my best friend from work? It has to be a mistake maybe he said Ella, but I knew what I heard.

He was fucking my best friend in my bed and she was fucking my fiancé? How could they both do this to me?

Oh god, is that why I didn't hear from him over the past two days?

How long have they been at it?

Shock had now truly set into my bones and I needed some air to breathe.

My hallway was spinning, my legs started to shake and I was hyperventilating and all I could do was head back the way I came in, through my own fucking front door.

Once I got outside the building I was sick.

Everything from the plane food and drink was flowing freely from my stomach and I could not stop myself.

Why?

I started to run and then walk with no direction in mind; it was late and getting cold.

I was not wearing much from my return journey but the chill was the furthest thing from my mind; I just had to keep moving. Tears were flowing from my eyes and every step I took blurred my vision, whilst my breathing was still erratic.

I took out my phone and called Rebecca, why I don't know but she was the only person at this time I could think of.

After a few mumbled attempts at crying, shouting and pleading with her to come and get me, I then had to figure out my location.

She came within minutes in her PJ's and slippers, and I just hugged her and cried hysterically.

"Jesus Autum what's wrong? Has your house been broken into? You look like you've seen a ghost, are you alright?

She could have said a lot worse or even thought it, as I know I must have smelt of sick and looked like shit. I could only hear the words that Rebecca was saying because it was going in then coming straight back out again. I could not talk and just sobbed quietly to my inner self. I tried many times on the short journey to her house to speak but the words kept getting blocked in my throat.

When we got inside, she sat me down on her sofa got a blanket and let me curl around her like a mother protecting an ill child.

Stroking my hair she told me that it would be alright. I needed to be sick again and as I shot up Rebecca directed me to the toilet.

"Are you pregnant?"

I washed my mouth out and started a hysterical laugh.

"Pregnant!" I laughed again but this time it was short lived and turned into more of a sob.

I went back into the living room and sat on the sofa when Rebecca bought me in a hot drink.

"It's Jack. He was at my apartment, he was with, with," I started to cry again. I could not do this now. The image of them both in my bedroom fucking, it just wouldn't go away, still too fresh in my mind.

"Don't talk until you're ready. I'm here whenever you want to talk, no matter the time, stay here while I make up the spare bed for you, and drink your coffee, sorry if it's too strong."

I told her thanks, as I wrapped my hand around the cup for warmth and comfort as if that could take away the pain.

I went to bed around one, thirty in the morning, and just lay there, staring at the ceiling, my mind blank.

Rebecca had given me a few pillows so I curled around one and hugged it for dear life, as the tears ran down my cheeks and dried on my face.

I could taste the saltiness when it hit my lip, my breathing was steady but my eyes were burning, a combination of the jetlag possibly setting in and the night I had just had.

After blinking a few times my eyelids were getting heavy and before I knew it I was in darkness, sleep had set in.

Jack was celebrating his birthday with his family and friends at a small hotel reception I had hired for his birthday.

We had just all eaten and the drinks were flowing and everyone was having a great time. There were around sixty guests in total.

The DJ had just started to get the guest to make their way to the dance floor and "oops upside your head" was playing.

Me and Jack of course got down on the floor with the crowd and started rocking forward and backwards and from left to right as if we were all in the boat, laughter could be heard all around.

The DJ continued with the classic songs, and then Jack and I slipped away and went outside to get some air.

It was nearly midnight and the venue was hired until one a.m.

We walked through the grounds and breathed in the fresh air.

"Thanks" he said, "I've had a great time and so as everyone else by the looks of things."

He pointed towards the exit that we had just come from and you could still see hands waving in the air.

"This was the best birthday present ever."

"Are you sure about that as I have not even given you your present yet?"

I bent over to kiss him as he pulled me into him.

We backed into an old tree where he continued kissing me; slowly he pulled my dress just up above my waist and started to pull down my panties. "Not out here" I said, "what if someone comes looking?"

"Well they will have a good show won't they" he said as he started to laugh.

63

I stepped out of my panties as he tried to unzip my dress.

"Turn around."

I braced myself on the tree as he unzipped me,

My hands slipping out of my dress with ease my dress heading to the floor.

The sharp air made my nipples hard and I let out a sigh.

His hands were now around my bottom, stroking it tenderly, then slapping it and I let out a yelp. Again he laughed, and then I heard him undoing his zip.

He started to kiss my back placing kisses randomly all over, then using his tongue to slowly travel down to the base of my spine.

"God this feels good" I said as my breathing became heavy.

He grabbed my left breast and told me to open my legs.

I did so without hesitation.

Before long I released my right hand from the tree and grabbed hold of his now semi hard errection.

Up and down I stroked from the tip to the base as he moaned about how it "felt good." He released my hand and I could feel his cock pressing hard against by bottom.

"Open for me" he said as I parted my legs even more. I felt the tip of his errection pressing slowly into me, that sudden burst of sensation, as I got ready to receive him.

He entered hard, and I screamed.

The pain and the pleasure both hit me at once making me wet almost instantly.

My hand gripped the tree harder as the force of him behind me was taking me over the edge. "Don't stop."

In and out he went, touching my clit with his fingers. I squeezed down on him making the impact tighter and he moaned. He was still working me with those fingers, tipping me over the edge.

I was so wet and he was so deep, but still I wanted more.

Harder and harder he went as I could feel the sweat coming off the two of us, the party long forgotten.

I was on the edge and just about to lose control when Jack cried out "come for me Isabelle, come"

I jerked before I started screaming, and screaming no, no you bastard my name is Autum not Isabelle.

He came harder and harder inside me as I tried to pull away.

"Stop, stop" I shouted "I cannot take it"

I was now being shaken, my shoulders going up and down, and I heard the muffled sound of someone's voice. Yes, it was definitely someone's voice I could hear calling out my name.

I opened my eyes and saw Rebecca.

Rage took over me as I grabbed for my phone. "Who are you calling at this time of night; it's four in the morning?"

"I'm not calling, I'm texting that bastard, and he's not even noticed that I left my case by the front door, which means they must still be fucking"

"Oh god Autum, I'm sorry"

"For what? Who knew that my fiancé and my best friend had been at it for god knows how long?"

But to do it in my own fucking house, well that just takes the fucking biscuit.

I sent Jack a text from my phone:

When you and that whore bitch stop fucking in my house and in my bed I want you both to get the fuck out and don't come back.

If you try to contact me or see me, so help me I will cut that fucking dick off and shove it in your mouth.

Tell that bitch that if she dares to look in my direction at work I will klll her, now FUCK OFF AND LEAVE MY KEYS.

Once I had hit the send button I breathed, it's over.

I curled back into Rebecca, close my eyes and drifted off to sleep again.

Chapter Six

It's always the ones that we least think about that tend to be the most caring.

As I turned over in the bed, I realised that Rebecca had left and it was indeed morning.

I started to stir as I smelled the food wafting through the bedroom door and my belly started to rumble in protest.

I got up and headed for the kitchen.

"Smells good"

"Thanks, you hungry?"

"Famished"

"Sit down and I will bring it over"

As we sat down to eat, Rebecca brought over poached eggs, bacon, waffles, beans, sausages and toast.

"Wow you really have been busy"

"It's just nice to have someone around to cook for other than myself, now eat"

I looked up at Rebecca, who was so happy about having an unexpected sleepover and all I could say was "thanks"

Rebecca looked up and smiled, which said it all.

As I went in for bacon number three, my phone started to ring which made me jump.

My heart started to pound and I started to get that sick feeling again.

I got up and looked at the screen, *Jack*. I felt light headed. It was eight, thirty, and he had just noticed either my text or my suitcase.

They had been in my house all night, sleeping in my bed until morning.

I ran to the bathroom to be sick, but all I could hear was the phone ringing then stopping, texts being sent, and the process repeating itself over and over again.

I returned and look at the screen. Eight missed calls and four texts. I held it in my hand as it rang again and then just threw it straight into the kitchen units where it shattered into pieces.

I looked up at Rebecca who didn't know where to look or what to say, so I just asked her calmly if I could have some more food, to which she responded with a nod.

Now that my belly was feeling fuller than it should have been, I asked Rebecca for a towel and a change of clothes which she went to get.

I stepped into the shower and let the hot water hit my face, with my head tilted up I stayed there, as if that would wash away what happened.

I finished washing my hair and came out of the shower.

Heading back to my room, I towel dried my hair and took a good look at myself in the mirror. *You need to go back home, you may not think it right now but it will all work out in the end just be strong.*

Who was I kidding? I needed to be strong.

Could I deal with this? I didn't know.

But I would make damn sure that they never saw the state they had left me in.

I finished drying my hair, put on my borrowed clothes, thanked Rebecca for everything and headed out the door. She tried to protest saying that I was not in the right state of mind. Well she had got that part right but I did not want to put it off any longer; I needed to claim back what was mine, *my apartment*.

It was a mild morning and it was nice to have the fresh air blowing in my face. As I walked I went over a thousand different scenarios that would greet me when I got back home.

Would *he* still be there? Would *she?*

If he begged me to take him back would I?

The questions went on and on in my head and before I realised, I had hit my road.

Staring at the front entrance of my block for what seemed like ages, I took a deep breath and headed inside, pressing the lift to take me to the second floor.

I struggled for my legs to move. I could see my door, but today it felt a million miles away. The more I tried to walk, the further away it seemed to get.

I was here, outside my door seeing if I could hear any sound of life but nothing.

I took out my keys but dropped them, my hands shaking like I'd been out on the piss the night before.

I tried again then turned the key. I heard the click of the lock and entered my hallway.

My apartment that I called home seemed eerily quiet.

I saw my suitcase where I had left it the night before.

As I walked I saw my bedroom door closed, *cannot face that yet.*

Walking into my living room I looked around. *My* cushions splayed on the floor.

Were they having sex on the floor?

Nothing else seemed out of place, and then I walked into the kitchen.

Bottles of wine and alcohol had been left on my units and there were dirty plates in the sink.

They couldn't even tidy up, yet another reminder that they were here, did he hate me that much to do this? He must have.

I spanned the kitchen area and headed back into the living room. I tried to sit down on my sofa but stopped myself half way down.

If the cushions were on the floor, could they have been fucking on my sofa?

My heart started to race and I could feel my emotions building up.

I was hurt, heartbroken and upset. I needed to sit down to think but I couldn't.

I felt that they were still there.

I could smell "sex" all over the room and it was making me feel sick.

I ran into the kitchen and got a knife. Why? Because I was angry. I needed to take it out on something rather than someone.

I saw the sofa and lashed out, strike after strike, my inner demon had taken over, but it wasn't enough.

I then moved to the cushions on the floor and one by one slashed and ripped them, the insides going up in the air. You would have thought I was having a pillow fight but nothing about this was fun.

Then as I looked around my living room, I felt that everything in there was laughing at me.

I picked up the lamp shade and threw it into the telly, knocking off all the books and smashing the ornaments on the floor. I was truly possessed.

I stopped only to breathe and when I knew there was nothing else left to break, but it still wasn't enough.

I headed for the kitchen where the bottles and plates were.

The plates came out one by one from my sink and I let them hit the floor. The bottles took the same route just via the kitchen cupboards.

"The Shining" entered my mind where Jack Nicolson wielded the knife as he went on a rampage in his house before cornering his wife in the bathroom. The only difference was that Jack and the whore bitch were not in there at the time.

I casually walked to my bedroom door, knife still wedged in my hand and kicked my door open, and in that split second it hit me.

"The smell"

It was so strong I was taken back, sex, sex and more sex. The bed, *my bed*, was still a mess. Did they panic after he read my text and scarper? I would never know.

My sheets were strewn half on the bed and half on the floor.

My bed still had that "sunken look" where there bodies had been.

There were two empty wine glasses on the bedside table with yet another empty bottle beside them.

I closed my eyes and recapped what I saw then charged at my bed with the knife.

Everything that was in my path my mind told me to *"destroy"* and that's what I did. By the time I had finished my adrenalin was on a high. It was then that I knew something wasn't right, I felt "funny"

I ignored the thought in my head and the fact that the room had started to spin.

By then, I realised my body was heading for the floor and I couldn't stop it.

Then I blacked out.

When I tried to open my eyes, it hurt. I tried to speak but only muffled grumbles came from within me.

I could hear voices but was unsure whether or not it was in my head. I did not know how long I had been trying to open my eyes for, but I fell back into my dark world again.

Rebecca was there in my dreams.

She was crying and being consoled by some people in white uniforms.

I was trying to tell her that I was ok, just a small knock to the head but she could not hear me.

"Dear lord, please tell me that I'm not dead, or in a mad house".

Panic struck me and I knew that I needed to open my eyes.

The more I tried the harder it got, but I could see some light.

Yes it was definitely light I could see.

I stretched all my face muscles to get my eyes open and now I could see what looked like shadows in the room.

I tried again to speak and heard my own voice all crackled but definitely mine whilst the shadows were getting closer and closer.

Yes they could hear me.

My eyes slowly opened wider, but my vision was still blurred. At least I could see amidst the bright lights.

I heard someone call my name and the word doctor.

I'm in hospital, what the hell did I do? And how the hell did I get here?

It took a while for my sight to really focus but once it did, I realised that I was indeed in hospital.

As I turned my head I could see Rebecca crying and saying "thank god she's awake". I then looked over to my left, and I could see a nurse and a doctor and someone else, Frank. I turned my head back to the centre as I felt the tears rolling down my eyes, too tired to wipe them away.

Rebecca grabbed my hand and told me that everything would be ok, and just to rest.

I garbled "what is Frank doing here?"

She told me that after I had left, she called Frank and Julian and told them what had happened and that she was scared in case they may have still been in the flat when I had got back, and that she was worried about me.

At this present moment in time, as Rebecca was filling in the gaps on what had happened, all I could think of was the way Frank looked at me in that split second that I saw him.

It wasn't pity or disgust. He seemed genuinely concerned, probably with my state of mind!

Rebecca continued, and I remembered the state of my apartment, the havoc and destruction that I had left.

Did they see all that?

How can I look at them knowing they had seen what I was capable of, the destruction that I had caused?

Would I still have a job at the end of the day?

What would Frank think of me now? Would he think that I needed a spell with the men in white jackets?

I tried to sit up but I noticed that my hand was bandaged up.

Oh god, did I try and kill myself?

I asked Rebecca what was up with my hand and she told me that I must have cut myself with the knife as I fell that I had some deep gashes but nothing life threatening.

I wanted the world to swallow me up, the thought of my days events being retold by Rebecca in front of the doctors and Frank. I could see them heading for that white jacket sometime soon.

How long have I been here?

"Just a night"

Dear god, was I that bad?

"You gave yourself a nasty bump when you fell; the doctors said it was just a precaution, gave you something to sleep".

That must have been some serious drug?

I had to get out, I needed to get home.

"Rebecca, please help me up"

"You're not going anywhere" said Frank.

His voice was sharp and to the point. I was taken aback.

"The doctors said that you need someone to look after you and total rest for at least a week and your place is not fit for the living"

I looked away, the image of my apartment coming back at me in 3D, compliments of my mind, another reminder of what I had done to my own apartment.

"Rebecca has taken over your projects until you get back on your feet"

I went to say something but he cut me off.

"She has been briefed on what she needs to do."

"But"

"No buts" he said, this time even sharper.

"I have arranged for you to stay at my lodge where you will have total bed rest and no one to disturb you if that's ok with the doctor. You will be checked over, and if the consultants say you're ok to leave, I will drive you there myself"

"But that was your break? I can't do that to you Frank, thanks but I will be fine once I get home, Rebecca can pop in and check on me after work"

"Rebecca cannot look after you". His voice was scary now. "So unless you are happy to stay in hospital, and I'm sure that they will need the bed sooner or later then my offer is the only one you've got"

"I am already on leave as you know and will stay out of your way I promise." His tone was softer now.

"The lodge is more than big enough for us both. I will get Rebecca to pack some of your belongings and bring them to the hospital for you to take with you."

"Is that ok doctor?" The doctor nodded

"Good, then that's settled"

"I can't leave my home"

"Yes you can, it will be sorted by the time you get back I give you my word."

Those last words that he spoke made me feel even more ashamed of how I had behaved.

My boss looking after me, how could I feel lower than I did right now?

He offered and I had no fight left in me to argue and Rebecca had now left to get my things.

I was tired and all I wanted to do was sleep, forever if possible, and wake up later for someone to tell me it was all a bad dream.

Chapter Seven

Can you ever repay true kindness?

After leaving the hospital, Frank carefully put me into his car as I waved Rebecca goodbye.

How would I survive the journey, what would we talk about?

I turned and looked at Frank as we drove off, and again he must have sensed it as well and turned to look at me.

"Are you comfortable?" he asked in a soft tone.

I replied "yes"

The journey was not that long really, just over an hour. I did not remember most of it as I kept slipping in and out of sleep.

I felt a warm hand on my shoulder as Frank told me that we had arrived.

My first impression was that it was indeed a lodge.

Not a bad size from the outside with a golf buggy on the drive which seemed to fit him perfectly.

"It looks nice"

Wait until you get inside.

"There are a few creature comforts to make it feel more homely"

Frank took my bag and we headed inside. As I entered I could see cupboard spaces to the right which

Frank opened before explaining that this was where the ironing board and other appliances were kept.

Walking a little more into the lodge I noticed that just to the left was a door which had a toilet and off that was a shower room.

This one had the latest gadgets, a massive shower head and all down each side of the cubical were smaller shower heads which continue all the way down to around your knees with different colours depending on what mood you wanted to be in, *nice.*

Next to the shower room was a glass door. On opening it, I saw that it was a sauna, not big but you could fit around four in comfortably.

Walking back to the hallway we then continued straight into the living space.

"Wow" The view as I looked straight ahead through the two big open windows was amazing. I could see the balcony and the golf course.

The living space itself had a well proportioned kitchen, white marble worktops and cupboards, American fridge, toaster, kettle etc., but no microwave, *interesting?*

It hosted two big leather sofas, both of which were chocolate brown, together with a flat upright CD player and a huge TV, *yep a man pad* with a large dining area to hold eight.

We descended down some wooden stairs which matched the flooring upstairs and there were three different doors off the hallway.

'This is the master bedroom' he said.

It had a big window again overlooking the golf course, king size bed, walk in wardrobes and a flat screen television on the wall.

The en-suite bathroom however was big; it was bigger than you expected it to be with double sinks, separate shower just like upstairs, toilet and a Jacuzzi bath that you could have a party in.

The other two bedrooms were of the same layout but one had twin beds, the other a double and both rooms only had a shower.

Frank showed me to the second bedroom and put down my bag.

'If you would like to settle in, I will call you when the food is ready, and if you need anything just press the intercom on the wall." Wow I did not even see that as I was looking around, there must be one in each room?

'Thanks, I think I will rest for a bit' and with that I was alone.

This would be my new surroundings for at least the next week. I unpacked all my clothes and cosmetics, settled into the bed, and before I knew it I was fast asleep.

I was on a night out with the girls and having a good time.

We were all laughing and dancing all fully loaded with alcohol.

My feet had started to hurt which is what happens when you wear new black four inch shoes and by the time we left the club my feet were so numb that when I took my shoes off, "big mistake" the throbbing I felt meant I was quite willing to cut off my own foot.

The pain didn't matter much though, as it was the best night out in a while.

When the taxi came, Isabelle and I were sharing as she was staying over for the night.

We had a spa day booked in the afternoon. Jack was also staying over which he did most weekends and Isabelle and Jack got on well.

We stumbled into my apartment at three a.m. making so much noise I was shocked the neighbours did not come out into the hallway to tell me to be quiet.

With shoes in hand, I said my goodnights and went to bed.

The next morning when I finally woke up at eleven a.m., Jack and Isabelle were already in the kitchen.

I could hear them laughing and I could here Isabelle screaming.

I walked in and they were play fighting.

"Afternoon Autum thought you were never getting up"

"Morning" I said back with my morning after breath.

"We have made some breakfast just help yourself"

I startled myself and woke up, they acted like I was the guest in my own home.

How come I never thought anything back then? Could that have been the start of it?

I just thought they got on really well?

How stupid can one person be?

I stomped out of bed too quick and felt the room spinning and let out a scream.

Before I knew it I could hear Frank's footsteps thudding down the stairs and into my room, his arms were around me in less than three seconds.

"Are you ok? I heard a scream?"

"Err yes; I got out of bed too quick and felt light headed that's all'

'Would you like some water?'

"Thanks, but I think I just need to go upstairs and get some fresh air"

It was only when I had reached upstairs that I noticed that Frank still had his arms around my waist.

As I watched television on the sofa, I heard a knock on the door and jumped.

'It's just the chef coming to prepare our dinner.'

'You have a chef that comes here to cook for you?'

'Well yes, I have been using José for years, he's very good.

A bloody chef, whatever next a maid to run his bath?

Frank did the introductions and José made his way into the kitchen to prepare our dinner.

I think deep down I was jealous. Why? I have no idea and no reason to be either.

Frank was the perfect host, making sure that I had enough pillows to prop me up; he kept asking if I was ok and if I needed a drink but then I would just snap at him so loud that even José looked up.

I could feel myself blushing and apologised. *Why was I being such a bitch, after all that Frank was doing for me?*

We were having steak, asparagus, boiled potatoes and a mixed bean salad, it smelt divine.

I helped Frank lay the table and asked José if he would be joining us.

Frank and José laughed. He said that he wouldn't be, but thanked me for the invitation.

As the food headed towards the table the aroma hit me and once we had settled in to eat, I thanked José for what he had prepared then dived in.

"Wow, this is amazing." The sauce that José had made complimented the steak perfectly. "So you like it then?"

Frank chuckled to himself. "And you have not even tasted his pudding yet"

"Pudding" I said like a child getting a treat for being good. "What is it?'

"Finish your meal first; it will be worth the wait"

The meal went down a treat and all I could smell was the pudding. At first I thought it was a chocolate cake which in a way it was, so I was not far wrong.

It was chocolate soufflé and all I thought about at that selfish moment was that this was going to be the best week off sick I ever had.

I tried to gather all of the empty dishes but Frank, and especially José, was having none of it.

I felt helpless as I just wanted to show them, in some way, that I could earn my keep.

Once the kitchen looked spick and span José said his goodbyes and I heard Frank say that he would see him in the morning.

We settled in for the night, watching some cheesy chick flick. I think he did it more for my benefit than his and we said our goodnights to each other at around midnight.

I sat up in bed thinking how lovely today had been and how awful I had spoken to Frank earlier. He didn't even complain, and in that split second thinking of Frank I felt that churning in my stomach again, that instant pain. *Why are you fighting what you feel?* I dismissed it instantly and went to bed, my mind playing me up again.

It was eight, thirty in the morning when I woke up and made my way upstairs in my PJ's.

Without thinking I was greeted by Frank in his casual black slacks with a white polo shirt that fitted him perfectly and José who was putting the finishing touches to breakfast fit for a queen, *of course*.

I noticed Frank give me the quickest once over whilst trying to be discreet, but again I had forgotten that this was not my apartment and I could not stroll around it half naked as my PJ's consisted of a skimpy top and shorts.

I quickly turned and headed for the table. 'Did you sleep well?'

'Yes thanks, was out like a light, the bed is really comfortable. And you?"

"I slept well thanks"

We both tucked into José's breakfast which matched any all inclusive buffet and then I excused myself and headed for the shower.

As the water hit my skin I felt totally relaxed, refreshed and ready for the day ahead.

I planned to ask Frank if we could leave the lodge so that I could take a look at the village. When I had finished, I headed back up the stairs and I could hear Frank talking to someone.

As I crept upstairs and remained hidden at the top, I realised that Frank was speaking to the office.

He was telling his PA to make sure that Isabelle was moved with immediate effect to the 1st floor in administrations. He said that Thomas was expecting her and that she should report to him straight away.

I smiled, *serves you right bitch.*

Then he asked to speak to Rebecca. I could hear him saying things like, "did you sort out the colour scheme she likes? Are the decorators booked to start tomorrow as planned?" He also asked her to confirm with him later when the furniture was going to be delivered and to make sure that she was there to oversee it all.

They were taking about me and my apartment. Frank said it would be sorted out by the time I got back but I never thought anymore about it whilst I was in the hospital or here. I had forgotten all about my place and the state I left it in.

Then I heard the word Jack which jolted me back to the present.

He was asking Rebecca if Jack had been in touch, *he must have rang the office to find out if I had been in?*

He then said to Rebecca "thanks for not saying anything. You have been a good friend to Autum even though she possibly thinks there are none left out there, I know you have only become closer colleagues since the trip to Miami, but she couldn't ask for more right now"

He then asked to speak to his PA again and went through his work schedule.

I then came up the stairs; Frank continued to talk to his PA whilst I was on the sofa and finished talking shop around five minutes later.

When he looked at me, he possibly realised that I may have heard the conversation beforehand.

"Did you want to do anything special today?"

"I would love to take a ride into the village" I said.

"I would love to take you there" he said whilst smiling. It was a short ride, no more than fifteen minutes.

When we parked the car, there must have been some international fete on, showcasing cheeses from all over the world along with other produce from that country.

You could smell it as you headed towards the town centre and all the different marquees were set up; it was great.

I spotted a French stall and wanted to taste the olive oils with fresh bread along with some cheese.

The olives came in all shapes and sizes. I even found myself feeding Frank some food which startled me at first as I did it without thinking. But Frank, ever the gentleman, took it in his stride.

By the time we had finished walking around the stalls and around the town centre we had been out of the lodge for five hours and were laden with carrier bags full of international produce.

We were peckish and decided to pop into a local pub for something light to eat.

'You're looking much more like yourself today' he said.

'I feel much more like myself thanks to you'

Now Frank was the one blushing and I started to laugh.

It was a sight I never thought I would see and it suited him. I felt guilty for laughing, why?

Because I felt relaxed for the first time and even though it felt right it also felt wrong or was I just being hard on myself?

Remember I've done nothing wrong it was him.
If you feel like having a laugh, then go for it.

I ordered a jacket potato with tuna and cheese and Frank ordered a cheeseburger and fries and we both ordered coke. By the time we had finished, it was nearly three, thirty in the afternoon, so we headed back to the lodge.

I was in a joyous mood when we got back; I gave José some gifts of fine cheese and olive oils as a "Thank You."

Once we unpacked what we had bought, I was feeling tired, but did not want to sleep downstairs so I lay out on the sofa.

Frank had gone to get me a blanket. When he came back and knelt down beside me to cover me, I lifted my head to prop up my pillow, we were literally a hair's breath away from kissing each other.

We froze for a moment then both pulled away as he put the cover over me.

I turned to look at him and said "thanks"

'For what?' he said'

"For everything" I then fell asleep.

Chapter Eight

How do you know when you're really in love?

Frank left Autum asleep on the sofa; he was sitting on the opposite sofa looking at her chest rising, the cover going up and down. He could hardly hear her breathe.

He recalled when she came up for breakfast that morning in her PJ's and how it had made him feel, *like they were a couple.*

He noticed that he was looking at how long her sexy legs looked in those shorts she was in, and that she had the most perfect breasts he had ever seen *in that skimpy top.*

Feeling a little embarrassed, he recalled her noticing that he was looking at her, and how she quickly made her way to the table.

What she didn't know was how he was looking at her nice ass and wondering if he would ever get the chance to slap it. Frank smiled to himself.

Until Autum's arrival Frank hadn't noticed how empty his life had been without someone to share it with.

To wake up, and see someone in the same room as you and to have breakfast with, was something he felt he was now missing in his life, something he now started to crave. She wasn't his and he knew that, but he also felt even more jealous that someone like Jack was quite happy to throw it all away for some fling, with her friend, of all people, and not realise how good he had it and how much Frank now wanted it.

Frank recalled when Rebecca had made that panicked call to him and how he had felt in that split moment after getting the call, the pains in his chest and how his heart had started to flutter, something that he had not felt for any woman before.

Part of him was glad that Jack had fucked up.

As far as he was concerned, it meant that he may have a chance after all or at least he hoped he would. He thought about when he met Julian and they entered her apartment. The first thing that struck them was that the door was slightly ajar.

Her suitcase was not far from the entrance and they could see straight into the kitchen.

"I think that's what drew our attention as we walked straight past what we now know was her bedroom.

As we stepped into the kitchen it was as if a bomb had gone off and blown everything up.

Most of the cutlery was on the floor smashed to bits, we called out her name as we headed back through.

The living room, once we got inside, was covered with feathers everywhere, the sofa was totally destroyed, the TV smashed to bits, there was nothing left untouched in that room. Me and Julian just gave each other a look that said what the hell happened in here?

I started to panic thinking that Autum had been involved in some sort of fight and may have not come out of it unscathed.

This was destruction on a new level but who had done this?

Did Jack leave this as a reminder for her when she got home, maybe he did?

All I know is that Autum was still missing.

We then walked back to the room we missed on our way in. I tried to push the door open but something was blocking it.

I pushed my head in to look around the door and that's when I found Autum lying face down, blood seeping from her, a knife in her hand.

I squeezed myself through and called out her name again but still no reply.

I told Julian to go and call for an ambulance while I saw if she was still breathing.

I knew that once Julian had left and I was alone with her, how she had made me feel. I raised her head onto my lap and it was then when I looked down at her that I knew no matter how much I denied it to myself, I was falling in love with this women. It was instant and unmistakeable, and the fact that she would never love me back was something I didn't need to think about, my heart sank for this woman because she would never know how she made me feel inside.

When Julian came into the room his first reaction was of the carnage, something which, when I look back, I did not realise at first.

The bed, sheets and everything which was not nailed down was smashed, broken, and destroyed.

Did she corner them in here? Did they corner her in here I will never know?

For now, I was here for her and that was all I could have wished for, anytime that I spent with Autum would be precious, she was only mine for a week, and the days were disappearing too fast.

I also knew I was living in cuckoo land and if she did not like me before I had no chance now, she saw me as her boss nothing more. I would in time, watch her date someone else knowing that I let my guard down and told her how I felt about her in Miami.

Yes we've moved on, but should my gut still churn every time she looks at me or when I look at her? No it shouldn't but it does.

Then I think back to the hospital, she looked like sleeping beauty.

I held her hand for a short while, conscious that I did not want Rebecca to see me doing this when she arrived.

I stroked her forehead and pushed away strands of hair from her face. She felt so warm and soft, and by the grace of god, the doctor said that she needed total rest and someone to look after her.

God had given me this brief time of happiness. It may only be for one week, but this would be the best week I thought I would never have, and now, I don't want it to end.

Two more days and her house will be renovated; I just hope she remembers what I did for her when she moves on with her life.

Not as her boss but someone who really cared about her but couldn't tell her how much.

When she fed me today in the market place she was smiling at me, she made me feel like we were together, just another couple out shopping, *and I li*ked it.

I go through times when I am fine, but sometimes, like how close we nearly came to kissing today I felt jealous because she isn't mine, well, it makes me think that maybe we could have something more, if only she would let me in, I could never hurt her just love her.

I turn to look at her sleeping as she takes a deep sigh.

What could she be thinking of right now?

Chapter Nine

***Soft, gentle, kind, loyal and loving! Is there really a
perfect partner out there for us all?***

*I was dreaming about the day I had with Frank and
the days so far since I had been here, and they had all
been good.*

*I had seen a side of Frank that I did not see before,
but then again why would I? I had not been looking!*

*I cast my mind back to when we first had our close
encounter in Miami and how he told me how he had felt
about me for all these years and I smiled to myself.*

Why did I get turned on when he kissed me?

*I was shocked at first but then I started to enjoy
myself. Did I know then that something in my own life
was wrong?*

*Maybe, but why did I then keep thinking about him
and me "doing things."*

*Was that just my naughty mind playing games? Most
likely.*

*And why do I also melt at times when he looks at me
in that way.*

Was my mind asking me if I wanted more of him?

But I discounted those feelings as not natural.

*They couldn't be, I was engaged to someone else and
I should only have had those feelings for him.*

Frank was so loving and kind, so why had he not found anyone to share his life with?

Would I be jealous…….I found myself saying yes I would.

I felt so torn inside. Jack did all those things to me with someone who was close to me and I needed closure.

Why, because I truly wanted to move on.

Did that mean I loved Jack any less to do it this quick? No.

There were no excuses for what he had done. I thought of Jack now and felt nothing, just emptiness. My body was totally rejecting how he used to make me feel.

I decided that I needed to see him when I got back; they say that you should never look back and I didn't intend to.

Did I want something with Frank?

I didn't know? All I know was that I felt safe with him and deep down I didn't want to lose that.

Maybe we are just friends?

I hoped so at least. Could I give him more?

Would I want to give him more?

Only time would tell?

Today I wanted to kiss him and that shocked me.

When our lips were so close and I could feel the heat from him, I wanted him.

How would he have felt if I was the one making the first move, would it have been so wrong?

Yes, as I didn't know if I would be giving him false hope?

Frank had shown me how caring he could be, how attentive he is to someone, and I wanted that someone to always be me.

Had it taken this incident with Jack for me to truly find my perfect partner? At this moment in time I wanted him to be, but how could I want Frank so soon after Jack? This could not be rational behaviour. Was I just latching onto something which was not truly there? All I know was that I needed to think about how this may look and feel to Frank.

I stirred from my sleep to smell José's delicious cooking, again he had surpassed himself.

Wow, I really must have needed that sleep.

"Feeling better?"

""Indeed, I didn't think shopping was so tiring."

Frank laughed his haughty laugh and I laughed too. When we had finished our meal, I asked Frank if we could go for a walk.

It was a nice evening when we set out from the lodge but very dark being surrounded by all those trees. The air was sharp and I liked it.

'Tell me something about yourself Frank; I really would like to know more about you'

Frank kept on walking then began to talk. "As you know I am thirty, I was born in Oxford but moved to London at the age of eleven when my mom got a job in Canary Wharf.

I hated it at first as my mom decided she wanted a better education for me and sent me to a private school.

It was so different from my previous school, but after a few months I settled down and realised how much of an opportunity I had been given and thrived there.

I then applied to go to Eaton and got in and studied very hard the rest as they say is history"

'Do you have any brothers or sisters?"

No just me, there were times growing up I was lonely and wished my parents had more children, but they were both career driven. It must have killed them to have had me but I did not want for anything, and they truly do love me.

'Where are they now?'

"Both in the Bahamas, they have a small business that they run together and the rest of the time they spend socialising, attending charitable events and building up their contacts list.

I speak to them most days as they keep trying to persuade me to come over"

'You mean you have not been to see them?'

"Believe it or not no. Work has just been too busy and they keep asking me when I will be giving them grandchildren"

'So you want children then?'

"Of course I do, just not found anyone that I want to settle down with yet that's all."

'Frank, can I ask you something personal?'

"Sure."

"In your office there are lots of pictures of you attending events but you are never with anyone, why?"

Frank laughed, "oh that's simple I didn't bring a female companion with me as I didn't have one.

There were loads over the years that offered, but I knew that they wanted something I could not give them, and that was a relationship.

I thought about asking you a few years back but I thought better of it, I knew you had a boyfriend and by then I had started to have a bit of a crush on you" Frank blushed.

I stopped and looked at Frank. *He really had feelings for me all these years and kept them to himself until Miami, I didn't know what to say.*

"Are you shocked by my last statement?"

'A bit, you did tell me that you liked me in Miami, I just did not realise your feelings went back that far'

"Look Autum, I have always liked you and always will, you know that, well I hope you do now. I backed off because I don't break up relationships, and all you did at work when I had the opportunity to work alongside you or go on business trips with you was talk about Jack. Why would I try and ruin that? You were obviously in love"

OMG, he wants me still he's just as much admitted it, but how do I play it from here.

'It's not that I never liked you Frank, I just always looked at you as my boss, but then when you said what you said in Miami and then kissed me, well things changed between us"

Frank looked at me cautiously.

'What do you mean changed?'

"Well I felt angry at first when you kissed me but then I noticed that I was enjoying the way you grabbed me and held me close to you.

I started to respond because I wanted more of you, but then I panicked and ran because it felt wrong.

I was engaged and I shouldn't have let myself enjoy the kiss"

'You were enjoying it?'

I got embarrassed when he repeated my statement.

97

"I thought I overstepped the mark; I was so cut up about it"

"And I'm sorry I made you feel that way'

"I thought you would hate me, raise a grievance, leave the company, I was ashamed of myself"

I grabbed Frank by his shoulders and reminded him that he had nothing to be ashamed of.

I did not regret what had happened and before I could stop myself I was saying that I wished it would happen again.

Frank took one look at my lips and pulled me towards him, kissing me passionately. This time there was no struggle, no hurtful words just togetherness.

My lips parted and the warmness of our tongues sent shivers down my spine.

My hands moved from his shoulders to his hair gently massaging it, and then down to the side of his face, I did not want him to stop kissing me.

Frank moved his hands down by my sides and grabbed my waist, drawing me closer to him and a moan escaped me.

Frank knew his desire for this woman was growing and he could feel himself getting aroused, he starts to panic, as he remembers what happened in Miami coming into his mind and broke contact.

Franks breathing was erratic. He took in deep breaths before saying "it's late; we need to get back to the lodge"

'Did I do something to upset you?'

"No, oh god no, it's just I shouldn't have taken advantage of your words, you are still hurting.

I just find it hard to keep away from you that's all."

'Frank, this has been the best week that I have had. Yes I was hurting but Jack took the decision to cheat on me.

I never thought that it would affect me the way it did and I am ashamed about what he made me do to my apartment. He destroyed what I had built there, the memories, the fun. When I walked in on them in my bed, fucking like rabbits, I was sick to the core; I could not even react and left like a fool without doing a damm thing.

When I went back to see if they had gone and walked in and closed my eyes, all I could see was the images of them over and over again and I just flipped.

I could smell them, I knew each room they had been in, pictured scenes in my head, and it was only then that I realised that they had ruined what I had built up.

I could no longer look at my bed, my sofa, my living room without seeing them there.

I had to get that image out of my head, and the only way I could do that was to destroy everything I had, it was my way of dealing with it.

I hate him and that whore, for doing this to me, my fiancé and my best friend, what are the odds of that?" I laugh like a madwoman in front of Frank.

"It's always the ones you least expect, you know it happens to others but you never dream that it could happen to you.

Do not regret kissing me Frank, when I kissed you, I was kissing you no one else.

I was not doing it for revenge that's not my style. Am I still hurting? Yes, but for different reasons.

But that kiss, that kiss was real, I hope you believe that"

I stormed off, not angry at Frank but with how Jack had again made me feel.

Once I got back to the lodge I went downstairs to my room, slammed the door, flung myself on the bed and started to cry.

I could hear Frank coming downstairs as I tried to stifle my noise.

He knocked, but before I could tell him to go away he came right in.

I curled myself into a ball and faced away from him towards the window.

'I didn't mean to upset you Autum'

"When I was kissing you I had flashes of Miami and I panicked that's all. Call me silly or stupid or both. I have waited for you all these years and I want to make sure that when we get back to normality that you still have these, well these feelings for me if I can call them that.

I am happy to wait if I think that you truly want me, that you want us to be together"

I turned around so quick I nearly gave myself whiplash.

'Frank, when I am with you, you make me feel things I shouldn't feel.

My stomach goes kind of gooey and I get heart palpitations.

I have felt it a few times but dismissed it as nonsense"

Frank laughed

'I would never have thought anyone could go gooey over me, especially you"

Listen Frank, I cannot explain what I am going through; all I know is that if I am being honest, I don't want to lose you.

I started feeling this way since Miami; maybe you triggered something deep inside of me I'm just not sure.

Let's just see what happens when we get back" with that, Frank gets off the bed, kisses my forehead and says; let's see what happens when we get back home.

Chapter Ten

Whoever thought of the saying "whatever doesn't kill you makes you stronger", surely knew what they were talking about.

Before I knew it, we were packing up and getting ready to leave.

I said my goodbyes to José after breakfast hoping that I would get the chance to see him again.

I had the most peaceful night's sleep in a long time. No dreams haunting me, maybe because I felt that me and Frank were turning a corner and as far as Jack was concerned, well, not even a thought of him or that bitch had entered my mind, which was a first.

Frank had spoken to Rebecca a few times whilst I was checking that I had not forgotten anything and seemed pleased with her for what she had done.

Maybe my apartment had been fixed? I thought to myself.

Could I face going in after how I left it? This was another hurdle I would soon be facing and also I promised myself that I needed closure with Jack.

Our journey went by too quick. We had been talking about the weather, future business trips, and in fact I noticed we talked about everything except what would happen when I got home.

Frank was avoiding the subject and I was glad to a point, I just wasn't ready.

When I started to recognise familiar streets and shops, and the passing of our work building I knew that in less that ten minutes I would be home. Frank felt it to as he gave me a quick reassuring look and told me that everything would be fine.

The car pulled up outside my block and then I realised I did not have my keys to get in. 'Rebecca should be waiting for us upstairs'

Oh, ok, I started to shake, as my memories came back to haunt me.

My breathing was loud and choppy; I leant onto the wall for support as I started feeling light headed. Frank grabbed hold of me and held me the rest of the way.

Frank knocked and Rebecca opened the door to welcome us with a huge smile on her face, when she saw how I looked, she just helped me inside.

I stopped in the hallway and could smell fresh paint *he's decorated?*

I slowly went through the living room and was taken aback.

Gone was my leather sofa but replaced with a white one with a thin black border surrounding the edges?

My carpet was replaced with dark wooden flooring that complimented the living space and furniture.

I now had a flat screen TV embedded into my wall so big it took up the whole space.

As I continued to span the room, there were art paintings, a mini hi-fi, and wall lamps each costing a pretty package I guess?

With my mouth still open I was guided into the kitchen, the units were a shocking red.

All appliances built in, all new cutleries, dinner sets, kettle, microwave, toaster and even a new dining table. I was sure that there were even more hidden things in the cupboard like a dishwasher etc.

I could feel myself welling up, unable to keep my emotions at bay.

I turned to look at Frank and Rebecca and once I saw the looks on there faces I put my head in my hands and started to cry.

Rebecca gave me a hug and asked me "are you upset with the colour scheme?" I looked up and said it was more than I could ever have wished for and I didn't know how I could repay them.

Frank walked over and said "it's my gift and I do not expect any type of payment back." Rebecca then led me to the room that I had been dreading the most, my bedroom.

It took awhile before I could open the door, so Rebecca opened it for me.

My walls were white with the exception of a feature wall which was painted; they told me that the colour was called Caribbean blue.

The bed was at least five feet, with a high headboard in the same colour as the featured wall, with all accessories matching.

I also had a flat screen on the wall, floor to ceiling wardrobes, and dressing table. Every trace of what my old bedroom used to look like was gone.

It felt as if I had just moved into a new apartment, it looked, felt and smelt good.

They had even re-decorated the bathroom and the spare bedroom.

Rebecca had even put lilies in the kitchen and living room; she must have known they were my favourite.

After all the inspections were done, I asked if I could have a word with Frank in private, and without a backward glance Rebecca was gone.

'Before you say anything Rebecca helped me with some of the colour schemes it wasn't all my doing.'

'I love it Frank, it's beautiful'

But you shouldn't have spent all this money on," but he didn't let me finish and cut off my sentence.

"I wanted to. I could not have you coming back to your apartment the way it was, full of bad memories.

Would you want to be reminded of that day every time you came home?

I just thought a fresh look would help you try and forget that's all"

As I leaned over to kiss him, Rebecca returned 'oh, sorry, I forgot to mention two things:

Your locks have been changed just in case err you know.

And I would like you to come over to mine for dinner, can't having you cooking on your first day home"

"Thanks, I never thought about food"

'Well I have stocked up with lots of your favourite things that I noticed you had before, and when you're settled, I will show you how the appliances work."

"Ladies, let me take you both out for dinner, it is the least I can do especially you Rebecca for overseeing all of this.

You have done a great job and I won't forget it, I will pick you up at seven"

When Frank left, I felt like Mary Poppins. I stretched my arms out and spun around in my living room.

I grabbed Rebecca and with a squeal lifted her up and hugged her and told her thanks, over and over again.

'I know it's none of my business and you can tell me to do one, but you and Frank?'

I smiled. "There is no me and Frank Rebecca, that's the truth. He has been very good, kind and supportive to me and treated me like a delicate china doll. We got on very well and maybe in time…"

'Enough said. You look good together, just never looked at you both in that way before, but there is something that I need to tell you. I don't want to be the bearer of bad news but Jack has been ringing work"

'Yeah I overheard Frank talking to you the other day and guessed as much.

Do you still have my phone?"

"Yes it should still work, here you go"

'Tell me you are not going to ring that bastard?'

"I have to; I need closure to be able to move on"

'Do you need me, just in case things get nasty?"

'Thanks Rebecca, but I think I can handle this"

Looking at my phone I had in total twenty, three missed calls and seventeen, missed messages.

I did not read or listen to any of them but just dialled his number.

After a few rings I heard his voice and felt my heart racing.

'Hello, is that you Autum?'

"Yes it's me"

'Thank god, where have you been? I've been going out of my head with wor...'

I cut off his words as I did not want to hear them.

'We need to talk, are you free tomorrow around six'

"Yes of course"

'Then meet me at the coffee shop down the street you know which one"

'Yes I'll be there, how have you..."

I cut off the phone, my head pounding and my breathing erratic.

My first hurdle out of the way, how will I be able to tell Frank, will he trust me enough to do this without help, closure that's all I'm asking for.

We met Frank downstairs for seven and he took us to a lovely Chinese restaurant.

I played around with my food and thought that Frank realised something was wrong.

He kept trying to give Rebecca the eye to find out what was going on so I just blurted it out.

'Just to let you know I have decided to meet up with Jack tomorrow at six"

Frank looked over at Rebecca, who then shrugged her shoulders back to him, as if to say, I tried to talk her out of it, and then he looked at me.

His face was going a slight shade of pink and I know that look, *he's angry.*

'Is that wise?'

"Yes, I needed some closure and the sooner I do this the better".

'And if you don't get closure?'

"Then I will deal with whatever comes my way"

As I continued playing with this delicious food that should have been in my mouth, Frank's words played on my mind.

I never thought about not getting closure, what would happen to me if I wasn't going to get it?

He was a two timing cheat and after tomorrow I would never need to speak to him again. What could go wrong!

We left the restaurant at ten, thirty, and I said my goodnight to Rebecca as Frank dropped her home first.

Prepare to face the music!

The small drive back to my apartment was in silence. 'Will you come up?"

He did. I made him a drink and we sat down.

'Listen Frank, I can tell you're not happy, and it may be hard for you to understand especially with what I went through but please let me just do this one thing"

'It was just a shock when you said it at the restaurant that's all.

I know you need to do this; I just hope you don't come out more damaged than when you went in"

What did he mean by that?

This was going to be my first night in my new and improved apartment but with the evening's events, I started to get uncomfortable knowing that Jack knew I was probably back and that he may come round not wanting to wait until tomorrow.

I needed Frank to stay the night, but would he now that he knew what I was planning.

How could I ask him now?

109

Should I just explain that I feel scared? I bite the bullet and asked him anyway.

"Frank, you can say no if you want but…"

"You want me to stay over?"

"Err yes, how did you know?"

"Just a feeling I got when you asked me to come in. At first I thought you may have asked Rebecca being your first night here alone, but when I dropped her home well I just presumed.

'So will you stay then?'

"If you want me to, I will need to go home and get some things"

'Please don't go'

The statement came out rushed and I started to panic as I grabbed his arm for dear life, he sensed it.

Get a grip, why am I feeling this way, I have nothing to be afraid of?

'Are you ok?

I couldn't let him go and moved closer to him.

'Just don't go please'

We cuddled together as I wrapped myself into his warm embrace on the sofa.

His heat and the fact that I now felt safe sent me off to sleep.

I must have been restless in my sleep and knew that my heat source had gone. When I opened my eyes I was in my bed; *I didn't even feel him carry me there.*

I quickly climbed off my bed misjudging how high it was and the distance to the floor and nearly toppled over *damn.*

I went into the living room and there he was, asleep.

His jacket was folded over the sofa, his shirt buttons undone and his sleeves rolled up.

I walked around for a better look, he was breathtaking.

Just imagine waking up to that every morning.

His chest wasn't hairy but had enough fine hairs for you to run your fingers through it.

Why didn't he just sleep in the spare room?

I looked at his hair as he slept. It had that "I've just been shagged look" as he rested it on the cushions.

I went back into the spare bedroom to get him a blanket, but before I put the cover over him, I took a good look at this handsome man lying before me.

I bent down and whispered 'don't give up on me Frank, I want you, and I hope you want me' then kissed him gently on his cheek before going back to my room. What I didn't realise is that once I had stepped out,

Frank opened his eyes.

It was six, thirty in the morning and I needed to get ready for two big events, going back to work and meeting Jack.

Whore bitch was now on a different floor so our paths should not cross.

When I went into the living room Frank was not there, but I could smell something coming from the kitchen. He was preparing breakfast.

'Hungry?'

"Yes, but I never thought you could cook you know with José"

Frank laughed. "I can cook breakfast you know I am not that useless, and anyway I couldn't get my cook to come over" 'Your cook?'

He laughs again. "Only kidding," I laughed too. Rebecca really did go all out on the shopping; there was enough food for a small army.

111

I had poached eggs, bacon and tomatoes with two rounds of toast and a latte.

'You should be the one resting; I should have made breakfast for you since you are my guest."

"Well, I usually wake around five and hit the gym before I go to work, keeps me alert for the day ahead"

"Five?" I say at the thought.

He laughed and shook his head.

He left to go home and to change for work, "shall I pick you up?"

'No I'll be fine'

"You're sure?"

"Yes thanks, will see you at work"

He kissed me on the cheek and left;

I stared at the door for ages then headed towards the bathroom.

I got into work for eight, and felt apprehensive going through reception.

I felt that everyone knew what had happened and was staring at me. The truth was that no one had batted an eyelid but right now I felt paranoid.

I said hello to Janice and Bob in reception then headed toward the lift to the fourth floor.

A few staff said hello and asked me if I had enjoyed my holiday, *holiday? I wish I'd known that, I would have been better prepared.*

"Yes thanks, just went home to visit the family," *at least I said home, which could be anywhere,* "but glad to be back," *and the truth was, that I was glad to be back.*

Rebecca came to meet me soon afterwards. *Holiday*

"We thought it would not draw any attention"
'Thanks'

I spent most of the morning catching up with my emails and office gossip.

Rebecca also filled me in on anything I might have missed; assignments etc. and the morning flew by.

I went out for lunch with Rebecca to my favourite deli and then stopped as I saw Isabelle heading towards the same exit as me.

I tried to find another way out, but there wasn't. I thought I could handle seeing her but I couldn't, not yet anyway, it was too soon.

I could feel myself getting angry and for the first time actually wanting to attack the bitch, but this was not the place or the time to do it.

I took a few deep breaths and with Rebecca holding onto my arm, I felt composed, *not worth it.*

Isabelle was smug as she headed my way *and I thought she was my friend as I laughed inside to myself.*

She held her head high as if butter wouldn't melt, showing no remorse, no guilt, the bitch.

As we came within arms distance of each other, I put on a smile and asked her how her day had been.

I'm not sure who looked more aghast Rebecca or Isabelle.

She stuttered and couldn't form any proper sentence just only to say it was great, *liar*

I continued to walk, but could feel that intense burning in my back, *yep! She sure was plunging that knife in, as I smiled to myself, one down, just one more to go.*

The rest of the day flew by and I started to feel uneasy. The incident with Isabelle took all my strength and now I would be facing Jack.

This was only a meeting, I kept telling myself.

If I could handle that smug bitch, he should be no problem, I was the one in control of this meeting, and would decide when I had heard enough of his bullshit to call it a day.

It was five, forty five and I phoned Frank to let him know that I was now leaving the office.

He had asked me how my day had been and I filled him in with the brief encounter that I had with Isabelle.

'Will you promise to call me when you can?"

'Of course and will you promise to come around later?"

'If that's what you want, then sure'

With that I hung up the phone, topped up my lippy, sprayed my perfume and headed for the coffee shop.

It was now six and I ordered myself a latte.

I thought that I might need that extra boost of energy when I saw him.

My heart was beating fast but I knew it was only nerves and after a few sips I could smell him, the aftershave I had grown to love so much.

I looked up to see him standing there, as sexy as ever and my heart fluttered. *Oh god this should not be happening to me.*

'Can I sit?"

"Of course you can" I said quite sharply and brought myself back to the reason why I was here.

'You look gorgeous as ever.' I didn't reply.

'How have you been?" *Bingo!*

114

'Well let's see shall we? I go on a business trip engaged; I make daily phone calls to my fiancé who I thought worshiped the ground I walk on."

'I do'

"Shut it!"

"We have the best phone sex ever, and then I come home early to find you fucking my best friend in my bed". "How the fuck, do you think I have been?

"Babes," "Who the fuck, are you calling babes?"

"You need to believe me when I say that I don't now what came over me"

'I think it was her pussy in your face'

"I was already staying at your apartment when she came over. She said that she had bought in a few supplies for your return and then she was all over me.

'And you really put up a fight from what I could see'

"It wasn't like that, I was missing you, she was there and it just happened"

He stretched out his hand to hold mine and I pulled back.

'Did you ever love me Jack?'

"I still do, you know that, why do you think I have been going out of my brain trying to find out where you have been? We've been together for three years, we plan to marry, have kids, it was just a mistake, one that I will regret for the rest of my life"

'You got that right'

'Take me back please. I promise you I'll do anything to prove how much I love you"

I looked up at Jack and saw his sexy face and I was starting to lose my grip on this situation.

I was now blaming her and not him, forgetting it takes two to tango.

This wasn't going to plan and I needed to change tact.

'Where did you have sex in my house, I want to know?"

"Don't do this Autum please, it doesn't matter"

"Where the fuck did you have sex?"

I shouted, a bit louder than expected and people in the coffee shop started to look up, heads turning towards us.

He started to whisper now as he went through what he had done and where he had done it.

"We did it on the living room floor and sofa, the dining table"

'Dining table?"

"Oh I get it; I'm not adventurous enough for you. We've never done it on the table but you have no issues doing it with that whore?"

"What can I say? She's a wild one"

"How dare you, I was feeling sick and a lump had started to form in my throat"

"Where else?"

"The bedroom". He looked up to see my response but I gave him none, still numb from his confession.

'I'm so sorry.'

I tried to blank it out. I wanted to know and now I knew, but hearing it made me feel worse and I was in a state of shock.

When I looked at his face, I saw him and her together.

I pictured them all over my house having sex laughing behind my back, I needed some air.

Tears started to form which made me angrier that this was what he had reduced me to as I tried desperately for him not to see me like this.

116

'I hope she was worth it Jack, you lying bastard. You say you love me but still you had time to fuck that whore over and over again in my house. Not once did you think of me. I bet if I never came home that night you would still have been at it behind my back. How long has this been going on and don't fucking tell me this was a one off or so help me Jack I will phone that bitch and get her over here to see who's telling the truth"

With that he panicked and stuttered. "A few months"

I staggered back trying to get up out of my seat.

"Months"? It's over Jack, I don't ever want to see you or that whore again and with that I slapped him so hard my hand started to sting, then I got up, and walked off"

I cried all the way back to my apartment, the flashbacks started to hit me once I entered the living room.

Was I going to relive this nightmare time and time again?

The walls may have been painted but the scene would always be there.

I wanted so much for Frank to be waiting for me when I got back.

I needed to tell him it was over and that I could move on with my life. As I reached for my phone to call him I hear a knock on my door, *thank goodness it's Frank.*

I went to the door and opened it, but before I could close it Jack burst in.

Chapter Eleven

Keep your friends close and your enemies closer!

Frank struggled to concentrate at work. He had meetings back to back and he needed to deal with the job in hand, but the thought of Autum and Jack meeting disturbed him.

She wasn't strong enough emotionally to see him this soon, all he had to do was woo her with words and she would take him back, *or would she?*

It took all his might not to bed her when he stayed over that night; but he wanted to do things right, he wanted her to tell him she loved him and just when he thought he was making progress Jack entered the picture again.

God! Was life with Autum always going to be this complicated?

Then he thought back to that night he stayed over. He had always been a light sleeper, so when he could hear light footsteps he pretended to still be sleeping.

He could smell her near him and it was so hard not to open his eyes; he wanted to breathe in her scent.

When he felt her breath by his ear, for a split second he nearly opened them, but then she spoke.

'Don't give up on me Frank, I want you, and I hope you want me' then she kissed me.

She wanted him, he knew that now, but how should he play this. Instead of going home like he should have, he follows her to meet *him.*

He wanted to see what he looked like, and as he watched people going in and out of the café he presumed the man that went in by himself must have been Jack, well a few seconds later it was indeed him.

He could see Autum occupying a table by the window.

If she ever saw him, how could he explain his actions? But he just wanted to make sure she would be ok.

As he sat in his car watching them, trying to look for anything to suggest that she wanted him back he saw nothing and that made him sign with relief.

They were talking as far as he could see for what seemed like ages, she looked ok I think, and I decided there was no need for me to be here, she looks like she has everything under control.

As I looked down to turn the key in the ignition my phone rang so I answered it, I only looked away for a split second and when I turned back around, Autum was standing and then I saw her hit him: what the hell happened for her to do that. *I wish I was a fly on the wall at that moment in time, at least I know that she truly has ended it.*

As I watched her leave the café she looked upset and was walking quickly, I turned back and glanced at the café to see Jack still sitting in his seat rubbing his cheek and that bought a smile to my face *no going back.*

She was on the opposite side from me now and as she levelled my eye contact she had indeed been crying.

The engine was now running and I debated on what to do, I thought if I leave it for a while I could say that I was working late and decided to pass by her apartment to make sure that she was ok.

I relaxed back in my car thinking that it sounded feasible when I popped around.

Looking at the café again I noticed that the table they were both sat at was now empty, I glanced around the street to see which path Jack had gone, but at the corner of my eye I thought I saw someone running into her street, *could it have been Jack* I wasn't sure?

I tapped my fingers on the steering wheel, but could not shake this feeling that something did not feel right, and with that I indicated to pull out onto the road.

Only passing by so I can make sure that she is ok, *working late remember?*

I still have her spare key so I let myself into the block and headed for her apartment.

I approach and I hear muffled noises and thought it was her neighbours, but once I reached her door and went to knock, the door was ajar.

"Not again"

Chapter Twelve

I understand now when they say love is blind.

When Jack burst in, my first instinct was just to run, but before I got anywhere he grabbed me by my hair and I screamed. 'What the hell are you doing Jack?'

"No one dumps me, no one"

'Please Jack you're hurting me'. He puts his hands around my throat and throws me against the wall cutting off my air supply for a split second.

"Just shut the fuck up or I'll gag you" He then continues to drag me through the hallway before stopping and starts to look around the living room. 'Well, well, well, didn't take you long to redecorate did it? I must admit it looks very classy, do it all by yourself did you?"

I did not answer him as he continued to drag me into the kitchen, 'nice', and then back towards the bedroom.

By this time I started to fight, why would he be taking me to the bedroom, unless?

He would never try to force himself on me would he? Not Jack this is just not his style he is just angry.

I felt sick just thinking about it, but I had no intentions of letting him get me in there so that I could find out.

I kicked him and he buckled but not enough to loosen his grip on my hair.

He then wraps his arms around my waist and picks me up still kicking. Jack uses his bodyweight to open the bedroom door then flings me on the bed. 'Whatever's going on in that sick head of yours you better forget it'?

Jack's eyes looked truly evil, his breathing was heavy and for the first time I was really scared.

He started to strip and I knew then what his intentions were, he was going to rape me.

All the while I was still trying to convince myself that he could never do this to me. Our years of being together must have counted for something. They say love is blind, but I must have been blind, deaf, dumb and stupid if I could not see that Jack had a dark side which he was now going to show to me.

I jumped off the bed and tried to head towards the door while he was trying to take off his trousers but he grabbed my arm, turned me around and knocked me back with a slap across my face.

'Please Jack'

He stared at me with the darkest of looks.

'I told you I loved you, I begged for your forgiveness but you threw it back in my face, so now I'll do the same to you"

I started to scream when he put something into my mouth, he then tries to lift up my dress, pinning me down at the same time.

I kicked him and he slaps me again, this time I saw stars as he catches the corner of my eye.

He then got off me and took off his belt, tying my hands behind my back nearly dislocating my shoulder at the same time, with the force he used. He was laughing at me as he went on.

'Just giving you one last fuck to remember me by'

My face is now embedded into my pillow and I was struggling to breathe.

He lifts up my dress, rips off my knickers, and before I knew it, I felt a sharp thrust as he enters me.

I screamed as the pain goes through me, the tears rolling down my face, *god, please help me, what did I do to deserve this?*

He continues his onslaught a few more times, moaning out loud. "This beats phone sex any day", he laughs, each thrust more painful than the last as I felt myself going into some sort of trance, a total shutdown, dead from the waist down, anything not to concentrate on the pain and the monster doing this to me.

I hear a voice. *Don't let it be Frank, please god anyone but him, he can't see me like this, please.*

'What the fuck' is all I hear to determine that Frank is now in the room.

I tried to turn my head more into my pillow, screaming my muffled scream.

I hear Jack say 'who the fuck are you? This is a private party.'

Then I heard a smack, as Jack's weight now leaves me.

'You sick bastard, "whack", try picking on someone who can fight back, "whack"

I curled up into a ball as I hear things being smashed around me, the scuffle of two men fighting.

'Let go of me you fuck' was Jack's reply.

The noise and commotion heading towards my front door then "slam" and the place goes quiet.

Frank comes back in, but as I felt his touch I screamed, it was only then Frank realised that something was in my mouth.

"Sshhh I won't hurt you, I'm just going to untie you"

He slowly reaches for the belt and loosened it. I quickly take out what he had shoved in my mouth and took in a few deep breaths as I pull back down my dress.

Frank covered me with the sheets then pulled out his phone and dialled the police.

'N...No' I said in between breaths, "I can't do that, please cut off the call"

The voice on the other end still repeated, 'which service do you require?"

Frank ended the call.

He went out of the room and brought me some water; too ashamed to look at him I drank it with my head down.

'Let me call Rebecca.'

"No; I don't want anyone to see me like this, I don't want anyone to know about this"

Frank left the room again, unsure where he had gone, so I called out his name and he returned.

'I thought you had gone?"

"No just running you a bath, I didn't know what else to do"

'If you feel uncomfortable Frank you can leave, I'll be alright'

'Jesus Autum, what sort of fucked up fiancé were you dating, is that how he gets his kicks!'

"How did you know I was here?"

'I didn't I was working late and thought I would pass by on the off chance'

Good back up plan.

'I'm glad you did, you saved my life', and with those words I continued to cry, well ball actually.

He came closer to hug me then backed off, unsure of what he should do.

'You're sure I can't call Rebecca, she can look after you if you need a woman to be with, if you know what I mean'

I looked up into his face forgetting about the slaps I'd taken earlier. He went to touch me and again I pulled back.

'I'm sorry I wasn't here to save you, I should have been" Frank was distraught.

'Don't do this Frank'

"I never thought it would end like this, I never thought he could do this to me"

"I didn't let him in, I thought it was you when I heard the door knock, by the time I realised it wasn't, he had already burst his way in"

I tried to move off the bed with the sheet around me, but with every move came pain. Frank put his arm around me to help me up, and this time I didn't protest.

He guided me into the bathroom and turned to walk away.

'Just call me when you need me, I will be in the living room'.

"I need you to help me get undressed, my arms hurt and I need to take my clothes off and get in the bath"

After some shaky hands, he helped me out of my clothes and into the bath.

I always pictured him seeing me naked, but not like this.

'Burn them'

As he washed my back I wandered what was going through his mind. Did he blame me? Would he still want me because right now I knew I still wanted him?

'Thanks, you always seem to be there when I need you'

"But not today"

"Yes today. You still came round, if you didn't" I paused and trailed off.

'And you don't mind me being here?'

"Of course not, this is not an image you should have seen and I'm ashamed you have"

'I need to ask you something, this might not be the right time I know but.'

'What do you want to know?"

'I need to know would this change, err, how you feel about me, you know, what you witnessed."

'For god's sake, of course not, how could you think that of me Autum, after everything I've done for you"

"Well you know, with what's just happened and everything else, I needed to know, I wouldn't blame you if you did, if this is too much for you just let me know"

'Ok but there is something that I will insist on, and I won't take no for an answer"

'Demanding aren't you?'

"Autum please"

'What is it?'

"You will not be staying here anymore"

It was now nine o'clock, and I had packed a bag with some of my clothes. Frank wanted me to take some more time off work, but I said no. I just needed to stick to a routine; I refused to become a victim.

128

What he did I would never forgive or forget but it would not ruin my life. Did I want to seek revenge? Of course I did, but then it would make me no better than that scum.

Frank insisted that I stayed at his house; he said it was big enough for us to still have our own space when we needed it, *heard that before!*

I suppose you could do that with six en-suite bedrooms, acres of land, gym, steam room and a swimming pool. All that space for just one person?

He may be glad of some company then.

It was kind of how I pictured it to be, automatic gates with CCTV and intercom access. A driveway so big it took minutes to reach the house instead of seconds.

The big house itself had lots of windows and a sweeping landscaped garden. Just looking at it you could sense the peace and tranquillity which it gave you within the surrounding trees.

'You're sure this is big enough for you?'

He laughed, 'Well as long as you don't fill one bedroom with clothes and another with shoes, this will do me just fine'. We both laughed.

We went through the big double doors and immediately we were greeted by a lady.

'Hi Rosetta'

'Mr Lucas'

'This is my guest Autum she will be staying for a while"

Am I?

"Could you show her up to the guest suite?"

'Of course, will you follow me?'

I looked at Frank with a quizzical look and did as I was told.

We went up the sweeping stairs and along the longest corridor I had ever seen, if it wasn't in a straight line, I could have gotten lost.

My room was the furthest down the hallway. Once inside I could not believe it. It was the size of a house. The living space, if I could call it that, was huge. Sofas, built in TV, and all the latest gadgets.

Why would anyone want to leave this room?

Then off into another room was the bedroom with a bed so big I think it was made for the incredible hulk.

Walk in wardrobes *shoes!!* Then through another archway was the bathroom. Yep, made for the incredible hulk, twin sinks, separate walk in shower that alone was the size of my bathroom and robes hung behind the door so thick and plush you could use them as blankets.

I forgot that Rosetta was still in my room after I had done my tour.

'If you need anything miss'

"Please call me Autum"

'If you need anything Autum, you see that intercom over there, press it and speak' Thank you, *Frank and* his intercom systems. 'Would you like me to cook you anything in particular to eat?"

"Whatever you have, thank you" and with that she was gone.

After I had unpacked I made my way back downstairs wondering which room Frank was in.

Once I hit the hallway, I looked around to see lots of doors, twists, turns and archways, and I was lost. I called out his name not knowing where he was, and he came not long after from the room to my left. 'Sorry I was just in my study, did you manage to unpack?'

"Yes thanks" Good, now let me show you around.

Chapter Thirteen

How long can happiness really last? And where did the saying "too good to be true" come from.

I had been staying with Frank now for three weeks and we were going through that getting to know each other stage.

What I mean by that is we talked about what we liked and disliked, our favourite all time films, places of interest, the list goes on.

Since I had "temporarily moved in," most nights I had been having dreams about what went on with Jack, but the ones lately had been getting worse.

I had been scared to mention this to Frank as I didn't want to spoil things or make him any more protective then he already was.

We had been going into work as normal but I asked him to drop me off not far from work as I didn't need any hassle about people seeing me with him at the moment, but Frank thought that I was overplaying things.

Rebecca had been a rock and we were now great friends, we had girlie nights in at her place often, which is what I would be doing tonight.

I loved being at Frank's place but I also needed to see my friends and since the split with Jack I had not contacted the rest of the girls, Emily and Dionne. I promised myself I would do that tomorrow night.

My friends knew that Jack and I had split, that much I had mentioned, but they did not push for the reasons why. Work was hard today. I had to stay over until six, thirty to complete some important case files before a meeting with clients next week.

I did love my job but struggled today with my lack of sleep. Frank also worked late so that he could drop me off at Rebecca's, still cautious after all this time.

"Have you got everything" he asked.

"Yep, my overnight bag is bursting"

"Are you sure you're coming back? There are enough clothes and shoes for a weekend instead of a night"

I laughed, as by now he knew me so well.

"You can never have enough things. I like to prepare in case I change my PJ's or my clothes for work and if you change your clothes you need the right accessories"

We reached Rebecca's and he kissed me goodbye.

"Sure you don't want to come up and say hello?"

"I'm good thanks, enjoy," and with that I exited the car and watched him drive away.

When I got inside Rebecca's, she had her fairy lights all over her apartment, scented candles, the works. It made it so cosy and girly it was great. She got a chick flick movie and we had a great night in with a Chinese takeaway, followed by popcorn, peanuts and copious amounts of booze.

It was now eleven, thirty at night when we finally went to our rooms and I couldn't stop smiling. I hugged Rebecca and said "thanks"

"For what?"

"Because at this moment I don't know what I would do without you" she was definitely my best buddy especially when I needed her most.

I hung my two chosen outfits for work on the wardrobe, showered and went to sleep. That's when my dreams started again.

I was working late as usual and told Frank to go home and I would let him know when I would be leaving. It was around six in the evening when my office phone started to ring but every time I said "hello" there would be a pause then the line would go dead.

After the fourth time I shouted "either speak you fucking moron or don't call back". Then I hung up.

On the fifth ring he spoke "fucking moron am I now?"

"Is that you Jack?"

"You better watch your back bitch"

"Get on with your life Jack, I'm not interested"

"We can see that"

"What do you mean we? Are you with Isabelle?"

"Don't worry your pretty little ass, as next time pretty boy will not be there to save you"

And with that I hung up, and took the receiver off the phone.

Heart pounding and scared to death I rang Frank and he picked me up. Too scared to meet him downstairs he came and collected me in the office, a total wreck.

I woke up sweating, only a *dream*, but why did I feel there was a message in there somewhere. What? I didn't know, I was not even superstitious, but I was just getting these vibes I could not dismiss.

I got up and went into Rebecca's room and asked her if I could stay with her. She looked at me puzzled and asked what's up and I told her all.

"And what has Frank said to these dreams?"

"Not told him, I thought he would think I was being silly and paranoid?"

"Paranoid or not, he needs to know, they're obviously scaring you, otherwise you would not want to kip with me. Promise me you'll tell him or I will"

"Promise" and with that I crawled behind Rebecca in bed and fell fast asleep.

The next morning I was wide awake, feeling better for a decent amount of sleep. Rebecca was already up and from the smell again, she was in the kitchen.

"Morning, how are your feeling today?"

"A lot better thanks to you and before you say anything I promise to tell him today"

"Good, now get some breakfast down you and hurry up, can't have the boss moaning about you being late for work"

The breakfast as always was delicious; I hurried my shower and quickly washed and dried my hair and put it up in a bun.

We got to work and in reception were Jack and Isabelle. I was so shocked *only a dream remember.* I literally came to a standstill before Rebecca moved me on. "Don't rise to it." I was getting chest pains and felt like I was going to have a panic attack. They both stared at me with every step I took. Rebecca told me not to look but it was hard, their eyes never leaving mine and then that "smirk" from Jack. *You better watch your back you bitch*, that's what my dream had told me, and now I felt it was true, he was out to get me.

I reminded myself that he was the one that caused this situation in the first place but I knew I would be the one paying the ultimate price.

"Ignore them" said Rebecca as I smiled it off.

"Already done" which was a lie? We continued to walk as we went our separate ways to our offices.

It was now noon and I asked Frank if we could meet up for lunch. He had a prior engagement but cancelled when he realised I sounded upset.

"Has something happened"? I paused before I said "It's Jack," I think he's after me?" With that, Frank met me outside and we went for a walk.

I didn't plan to tell him about my nightmares even though I promised Rebecca, but now I truly felt scared and unprotected, and maybe I shouldn't have mentioned to Frank that it was Rebecca who had told me to tell him.

Frank flipped and I jumped. It was so unexpected that it caught me off guard.

"So let me get this straight" he said. "You have been having these dreams while staying with me, but said nothing and you are only telling me because Rebecca forced your hand?"

"It's not like that"

"What is it like then?"

"I thought they meant nothing, we all have dreams, some good, and some bad throughout our lives and that's what I boiled it down to". When I saw Jack today and he gave me that look, I just freaked out and tried to link it, that's all.

"Do you want me to have a word?"

"No. I want nothing to do with him and his mind games; I'm just a little on edge that's all"

We walked to a café and got a bite to eat before returning to work. I felt loads better and told Rebecca that Frank knew everything

When we finished work and we were on our way home, I stared at him, not knowing what was going through his mind. "Sorry Frank." He gave me a quick glance and placed his hand on my knee.

"Just don't shut me out, no matter how silly you may think it to be, let me know ok, I worry about you that's all"

"Promise" and with that he smiled and we continued our drive home.

Rosetta greeted me with a letter in hand. "This is for you Autum, but I was not expecting anything so Frank took it from me to inspect the envelope. "Oh it's from the estate agents, I hope you don't mind but I put your apartment up for sale.

I told you that you will not be going back there and I meant it, these are all the details, take a look and let me know if you are happy with what they have done"

I took the envelope and retired to my room, "For Sale" with a picture of my apartment from the outside and then all the features inside of it. I looked at the pictures and it looked so beautiful, brand new but unloved. I never got the chance to make it my home and that was my only regret.

When I saw the picture of my bedroom I froze, those dammed images coming back into my mind. I blinked them away and looked at the asking price, £225,950.

"Wow" was it worth that much? I had bought it four years ago off plan so got a good deal then. If it sold for this much I could pay back what I borrowed and put a nice deposit down for another one. I loved being here with Frank, but this was his home not mine, and I could not expect him to want me here forever even though I felt like I was part of his life now.

Since I had been here, we have not been "together" We kissed and cuddled but nothing more. It had been so hard for me to resist him when he had been so close to me, but taking my time with him had worked out better than I could have asked for. He was my friend and now I was relaxed with him I was ready to take things to the next level. I just hoped he still wanted me.

When we had been close on the sofa and cuddling, I would sometimes stroke his leg when we watched a movie, something I did automatically. I noticed him getting aroused, his breathing deep, but he was trying to control his urges, so he would quickly get up and say we needed some more food or drink from the kitchen and I would chuckle to myself.

I went back downstairs and told Frank that I was more than happy with the valuation and that he had captured all the details. He also told them to include "All" fixtures and fittings. I told him that he had only recently redecorated and paid a lot of money for it but he said that I didn't need them.

I felt bad and promised to give him some money to cover the loss of these items once the sale had gone through.

We talked about going back to collect some personal items, but this made me jitter.

"You won't be by yourself, I'll be there". I smiled and felt re-assured.

Friday came around and I kept my promise and phoned the girls. They were both together so I had the opportunity to say what I needed to say and only had to say it once.

They were heading out on the town and they asked if I wanted to come, oh! "Maybe next time, I promise," this caught me off guard. I had not prepared myself to go out, and just wanted to hear their voices. We chatted for a bit, never mentioning "whore bitch" by name and that felt good. God I missed the girls but next time I met them I would introduce them to Rebecca.

I was now going to face another fear, my apartment. It had been so long since I stepped in there. Rebecca had been back a few times for me to collect some clothes, shoes etc. after I gave her a blow by blow account of where everything was, but now it was my turn.

Frank held my hand as we went in. It was weird in a way, being scared of your own space, but as I looked around, deep down I was already so far detached from it, besides a few personal things, it felt as if I was looking around someone else's apartment.

We both went into the bedroom together, bless Rebecca, she had changed all the sheets for me. I took a deep breath, not wanting to stay to long in this room.

As I started to collect some clothes and shoes, Frank said "leave them"

"But I need"

"I said personal belongings only, as of now, you will be having a new start, with me"

I was so shocked with that statement I had to ask him what he meant. "What do you mean new start?"

"I want us to be together Autum. I want you in our home, and also in our bed, I want you now and forever, no more separation"

He said our home and bed? He wants me, oh god he wants me? I dropped the things in my hand and went to him as he opened his arms to greet me.

"I don't want to lose you, please say you'll stay." I kissed him so hard he said "easy tiger" and I laughed. "Can I take that as a yes?"

"You sure can" I said as I kissed him again.

We got back to his house, sorry I mean our house, and I was still on a high. I felt I had everything that I could have wished for, thank goodness for happy endings.

After dinner I went back into my room and it feels weird that I would now be moving out of this beautiful space. He greeted me with a hug around my waist and I moved closer to him.

"Ready?"

"As I'll ever be," and with that I took the short walk to his room, sorry our room, *I love that phrase.*

How a house could be this big and have even bigger rooms inside I would never know. My room was elaborate, a house unto itself but this, this was on a grander scale. The master bedroom boasted a four poster bed with heavy draped curtains on each pillar, even higher than mine in height.

Two walk in wardrobes and enough shoe space to fit a whole shop's worth of stock, and the bathroom, this was huge, white and gold décor, twin sinks, the walk in shower and the jacuzzi bath that was sunk into the floor space.

"Do you like?"

"It's lovely, just takes my breath away"

I put my toiletries away and then headed back into the bedroom. It may have sounded funny but I asked "what side do I sleep on?" He laughed. "Whichever you prefer" he said before kissing me.

I put my PJ's under my pillow and headed back downstairs.

This was now a new set of feelings for me. I was ready for Frank and now I had him, I was scared of us being together. Time ticked by and it was now ten, forty five and he asked if I was ready for bed. I smiled as he took me upstairs.

Once inside he headed for the bathroom and I sighed in relief. I thought to myself, *this is what I wanted remember!*

Yes, I did remember and I decided to go for it, no time like the present.

I stripped off and put on a robe I found behind the door. I entered the bathroom which was now full of steam and saw Frank naked for the first time. My heart fluttered as I saw him from behind, his bottom small and firm, his back lean and his muscular arms waiting to grab me up in.

I took a step closer just as he turned around and saw me, and I stopped.

He stopped too and looked at me, the water bouncing off him. I could not help myself and my stare took in his chest then moved down to see his cock, long, thick and coming to life as I looked at it.

It started to rise in approval for me. I looked up again to Frank, undid my robe and stepped into the shower.

I placed my hand around his neck as I kissed him, the water hitting my face. I took his tongue as deep as it could go into my mouth as I swallowed him up. I put some cream into my hands and put the lather all over his chest, my first skin to skin contact, he removes my hands as he takes the cream and returns the favour, his hands lingering a few seconds longer around my breasts, I laugh.

His hands now around my waist, he pushes me into his hard erection and I gasped.

Without realising it, I was now backing into the wall as a burst of coldness from the tiles hit me. As I settled, he cups my breasts with his hand and fondles them, his mouth hungry for the taste of my nipples as he sucks and bites them, the water sending my sensation even higher as it hits my breasts. I loved it, wanting more.

He goes down on me and tells me to "open" which I did. He slides his hands inside my thighs and I could feel how wet I had become.

"Wider" and his husky voice sends sparks throughout my body as I put my hands on his shoulder to steady myself.

His tongue passing in-between my thighs as he gently licks my clit. I moaned so loud and gripped his shoulders even tighter never knowing where his tongue will go next.

141

He flicks his tongue over and over and I found it hard to control the urge to have an orgasm. "Stop please. I don't want to come," my breathing sounding like I had run a marathon.

He pulls up from the floor and I turned him around to the wall.

I did the same to him as I bite around his nipples, feeling the fine hairs. I flicked them with the tip of my tongue as they bounce, making them harder.

I pinched them with my fingers, giving him a little pain and he moans.

I also go down on him and tell him to "open" as he did to me, he puts his hand on my head for support whilst I licked the tip of his cock, I look up before taking it into my mouth, the length trying to choke me, the width trying to kill me.

In and out I went as he became harder and wider. I took it out and sucked the tip, squeezing his balls gently in my hand.

"Jesus Autum. I won't hold out much more myself unless you stop"

I laughed and rose to my feet, his cock poking me all the way up from my chest to my stomach trying to find an entrance.

He dragged me out of the shower panting. I yelped as he threw me on the bed. He was now on top and stopped to look at me.

"You're gorgeous" he said as I blush.

He parted my legs as he placed his finger inside me. I grabbed the sheets as he went in and out of me, adding another finger until he fully stretched me with three.

"You're so wet." I blush again as he removes them, and I felt empty in an instant.

142

He places my legs across his shoulders and pushed my bottom closer to his knees. I continued to pant as I got ready for contact, then he slid it in, slowly and I moaned. I moaned because it felt so good, thick and hard. I moaned because of its length filling my insides and because I wanted more, he was giving me all this pleasure.

He also moaned with that same feeling and bent my knees for deeper penetration as he tilted forward.

"That feels good" I said.

My knees were now meeting my chest as he lifts me up and thrusts even more. This time he doubles his speed, his balls hitting me like a freight train and it felt good.

I didn't have much longer to wait, I was so nearing explosion I could feel the build up taking over my whole body. A few more and I would be gone; he never slowed down, kissing my knees as he went on. This was it; I could take it no longer and came.

I let out a scream as my body starts to spasm, shocks travelling from my head to my curled up toes.

On and on my orgasm went, my moans making him harder inside, filling me, he too was ready to come. He tilted his head and came, pumping that warm flow into me over and over again until he finally had nothing left. Once he got his breath back he collapsed beside me.

We stayed on the bed for some time, nothing said but everything said at the same time. That was great but I wasn't done with him yet. Frank had just wetted my appetite and I was still hungry. We started to kiss for a while and he asked me if I was ok.

"Never better" I said, heading back to the bathroom to clean up as he followed me, the room still full of steam. We changed the soaked sheets on the bed for dry ones.

While Frank relaxed on the bed, I sat on the chair by the dresser and started to comb my hair through as it was starting to get tangled, me naked by the mirror.

"Stay there" he said and I did, puzzled as to why?

He turned me around and began to part my legs, in an instant I felt that buzz again, the thrill of not knowing what was coming next, down he went the gush of air and the heat of his tongue descending on me I positioned myself for contact and leaned back on the dresser for support.

I opened my legs even wider without even being told. *I'm such a naughty girl.*

His tongue slid inside, and by the time it came out I was wet as hell, no playing hard to get, just down right dirty wet.

When he flicked his tongue around my clit I was weak, still recovering from before, could I come again? Was it possible so soon after the first? I would surly find out.

With my legs as wide as they could go, I gripped the dresser for dear life, my legs started to shake every time he hit the spot, over and over again.

This time my sensation hit a new level, topped up from the one before, making this orgasm wilder, stronger and more intense.

Frank was doing this to me; he was taking me over the edge and back again.

This was intense pleasure, something I hadn't experienced before, and something I would be experiencing again.

Chapter Fourteen

Party hard, who would have thought it?

Frank had taken me shopping to buy some new clothes, shoes and underwear. I thought men hated that type of thing, but he enjoyed every minute of it.

When we hit the lingerie shop Frank's eyes went wild, the window display showing skimpy lace knickers and matching bras, G-Strings, thongs, the works. I knew we would be going in.

It was done out in a type of "Moulin Rouge" theme. Pink and black lace wallpaper, chandeliers, and rows upon rows of the sexiest underwear you could find. It left me speechless.

"Pick what you want" he said.

"Do you mean pick what you would like to see me in?" He laughed.

I looked around the shop, feeling the lace and satin materials and picked up an array of outfits from basques to suspenders, it was like being in a sweetie shop.

"Mmmm" he said, "I like this one." It was a gold satin bra set with a basque and suspenders to match; I picked it up and added it to the others in my basket. After trying the basque on and feeling the softness of the material and how it just clung to the body like a glove, I understood then the fascination of what makes people wear them, and who they wear it for.

On leaving the store three bags later we headed out for lunch. Rebecca had rung me to see if I fancied going out on the town with herself and Imogen, someone I had seen around work a few times. Frank said it would do me good so I agreed.

It had been ages since I went out and the more I thought about it the more excited I became. I also decided to ring Emily and Dionne and make it a proper night out.

Once we got back home, I spread all my new things on the bed and picked out an outfit and underwear to match. Rosetta had prepared a seafood stew with crusty bread which was ample as we had already had lunch. I wanted to relax before I got ready but I also wanted to try out different hairstyles, should I put it up? *Look like a secretary*, what about down? *Nothing new*, shall I straighten it? Possibly or shall I put ringlets in? I liked that idea, so ringlets it was.

After having a shower I wrapped myself up in my bathrobe and started to pack away all my new things, but it still felt strange walking into my huge walk in wardrobe.

Frank was working in his study so at least he wouldn't distract me. Last night I was scared of how our first night would be, but after seeing him naked in the shower, well that didn't last long; this brought a smile to my face.

He was good, I mean real good. The way he touched my body, how he moved his tongue around me, the thickness of his cock. For someone who had not been dating, he sure knew his way around a woman's body, god I felt wet just thinking about him, I couldn't ask for more. Well I could, but that would just be too greedy,

146

and I'm used to being a very greedy girl. I laughed out loud.

It was now nine, thirty and I was adding the finishing touches to my hair, and make-up. I was wearing my gold lingerie set, except the basque that Frank picked out.

I slipped on my little white lace dress that I bought with matching black shoes and bag and headed downstairs.

Frank whistled and I blushed. "You look amazing"

"Thanks to you" I said.

"Are you ready?" I take a deep breath.

"As I'll ever be" and with that we headed out the door and towards Rebecca's.

He dropped me off at the entrance and told me to enjoy myself and to come home drunk so he could take advantage of me; I laughed and told him I would see him later.

Rebecca introduced me to Imogen from work.

Imogen looked like a party girl, the one that can hold down her drink and match any man who thinks to take her on. She had mousey curly hair to her shoulders, beautiful brown eyes and a lovely figure to hold those big boobs of hers, and a little black dress to hold them in.

Her breasts spilled over the top putting her dress under immense pressure. They were just so big and I thought I had a good pair.

"Yes it's going to be a good night" Rebecca said as Imogen knocked back her third can of Carlsberg.

We hailed a taxi and headed into town. Not long after, we met Emily and Dionne and we hugged and screamed that girlie scream when you meet up with the girls. I introduced them to Rebecca and Imogen.

"You look amazing" they said in unison.

"Thanks"

"How have you been?"

"I've been fine thanks, but we're not here to talk about me, just to have some fun, right girls"

"Yeah" they all said. We headed into a wine bar to start the night off but Imogen wasn't feeling it, so we stopped for one glass and moved on.

We then started to check out most of the clubs and the queues to get in and settled for one that played a range of music. On paying our fee and entering, we found a corner and sat down and ordered a round of drinks, shots and beers for Imogen of course.

The music was loud, the place overcrowded but the atmosphere was buzzing and it was exactly what I wanted, all you could hear was us laughing, getting chatted up by blokes and dancing, it was great. Imogen made me laugh the most, I did not realise she could be so much fun. She would burp like a bloke, ward off any bloke who came too close but when she laughed all you could do was join in, it was that contagious. "Love you Imogen"

It was two in the morning and Imogen was in her element. The blokes brave enough to venture near her were treated to those watermelons she called breasts.

She was now drunk and was horny and started kissing a man she had just met, we all laughed as they put on a show, they were really going at it, her hands were up in the air dancing to the beat of the music, grinding him as she went along, his head was buried in her chest while his hands was trying to grab her ass, but Imogen would give him a slap now and then if he pushed to far, wow, this was better than stopping in any

148

day; at least she wore sandals and not high heels like the rest of us.

It was three, thirty by the time I got back home. I was truly sloshed after having ten shots, three whiskeys, four glasses of wine and a shot of brandy and baileys together; *I wonder who introduced me to that drink?*

I struggled to focus on the stairs but holding the hand rail I guided myself up.

I tried to be quiet but kept struggling to get out of my outfit; Frank stirred and came out of bed.

"Sorry didn't mean to wake you" I said as I slurred my words.

"Light sleeper remember"

He helped me out of my dress and then stopped when he saw what I had underneath.

"My favourite", and with that he kissed me. I knew then that sleep would not be on the menu tonight.

"Turn around" he said, and I did *slowly*, with my back away from him, I rested my hands on the bed.

I felt his warm hands caress my bra as he lifts it up and pinches my nipples.

His hands wrapped around my stomach then back up to my bra which he takes off, the sensation goes through me.

He cupped my breast in his hands and I felt him getting hard behind me. He pulls down my underwear and I stepped out of it, but as I try to take off my shoes he pulls my hand back.

"No. I want them on"

I was now naked except for my killer heels, my head bobbing up and down as I held onto the bed.

"Spread your legs for me". He sent kisses down my back and chills down my spine. He reaches around my front and starts to play with me but I started to wriggle as he makes me wet.

He slides two fingers in me aiming deep before smothering my outer layer with my juices.

I felt him naked now his cock, which was sleepy, was now ready to explore. It poked my bottom as hard as a finger and tickled me as I laughed, just gentle stokes up and down then around, like he was spreading butter on bread, I was now on the edge and needed him inside me, I was all worked up. I needed release and fast.

I pushed back but he pulled away. "Not yet" he said. I sighed and he laughed.

He then enters me from behind, solid as a rock as I tried to grip the bed for support but slip a few times *the alcohol taking its toil* but he was there holding me tightly around my waist.

I slid further down the bed for deeper contact, with the feeling of pleasure and pain *and alcohol* all at the same time.

He stopped and turned me around; probably a bit to quick and I felt my head spinning and my stomach churning, like an un-invited guest trying to spoil a party.

He lifted me towards one of the pillars so now my back was being supported, he used his right hand to grabbed my leg and lift it up, wrapping it around his waist, as he enters me again.

His trusts were fast and demanding, I liked it. My breathing was not as good as I still felt the room spinning. I put my hands around his neck then moved it over my head and held onto the pillar trying to keep up the rhythm going.

Frank was hot and sweaty, his skin clammy, he lifted up my other leg and I was wrapped around him like a cocoon as he carried me to the bed.

"I could fuck you all night? You turn me on so much; this is all I think about" he said as he moved underneath me.

I straddled him and his cock hit me with a new surge. I threw my head back, his arms at my waist guiding me up and down.

He opened his mouth to moan, and releases inside me. I followed soon afterwards, my pussy throbbing but still sucking him harder, not wanting to let go. I then collapsed on top of him. *Drunken Sex!*

It was nearly noon before I stirred my head worse for wear and my hair too shagged out to be helped. I patted it down and got out of bed.

I took a quick shower to wake up and dressed in a casual skirt and top leaving my hair natural to dry.

"Good night" he said with a smirk

"Very funny" and yes it was a very good night.

"Rosetta has left you some breakfast if you can handle it; get some juice down you I want to take you out"

"You don't have to you know, we can stay in, it's Sunday?"

He hesitated for a moment and I wandered what he had planned.

"Are we going somewhere special? If so just give me time to change"

"I wanted to take you out for lunch to meet some of my friends." This took me by surprise, I had never thought Frank had friends, I know it sounds mad but I

151

just never thought about it and now he felt ready to show me off and I felt honoured.

"Where were you meeting them?"

"At the golf range, but if you don't feel up to it I can cancel."

"No. Just let me change into something more suitable and pour me some juice while you're waiting"

"Didn't you have enough juice last night?" I turned to look at him smiling and nodded my head.

We arrived at the golf range and I wore a fitted pair of black trousers, blouse, and matching jacket and low heels. He held my hand as we walked inside; I felt more relaxed once he did that. As we entered a smile lit his face and I predicted that the two gentlemen approaching us were his friends.

"David, Peter. This is Autum". I smiled, as each one greeted me with a kiss.

"Please to meet you at last"

"I can understand why Frank wanted to keep you under wraps, you're beautiful". I smiled as I blushed with the compliment.

We sat down for lunch and the guys started giving me the third degree which I expected.

"So how did you two meet?" David asked.

"I've known Frank for years; we work in the same building"

"He's been a changed man over the last few months and that we owe to you" I wasn't sure if he meant that in a good or a bad way but I think my confused look made David continue.

"What I meant to say is that he hasn't stopped talking about you, you really have made an impression on him. He has never introduced us to anyone before which means that you are someone special. I think he truly is in love with you"

I looked over to Frank, who was busy catching up with the latest news from Peter. He turned and winked at me and I smiled back. How could I top that last statement? I couldn't, because if he did feel that way towards me would I be able to say the same thing back?

I had strong feelings for him, but I think I was scared to let myself fall for him totally. I was holding back, Jack's betrayal still fresh in the back of my mind, the man I had loved for three years.

All I knew was that my feelings for Frank were totally different from what I had with Jack. The way me and Frank are together was so different, I could not compare and I wouldn't want too. I probably did love him, but was scared to say the words out loud just in case things went wrong. After all it had not been that long.

The rest of lunch went by quickly and at the end of the afternoon we were agreeing our next date. Frank mentioned that he expected to see them and their partners at the next formal dinner and they shook on it before we left.

"I think they like you" he said.

"Thank you."

"They didn't give you a hard time did they?"

"No they didn't. They were just happy to be introduced to your girlfriend. They care about you a lot, that I can tell and only want the best for you, that's what friends are for.

You mentioned a formal dinner is that soon?"

"I'm sorry I didn't mean for you to hear it like that, it's a charity dinner for the young and homeless. I attend different charity events every year as you know

153

and this is one of them. I was going to tell you anyway as I wanted you to attend with me"

"I've never been to any type of formal function before, would I need a gown?"

"Yes you would, but don't worry about that now, we have plenty of time, and it's not for another three weeks yet"

"Frank, don't take this the wrong way, but don't feel that you have to take me.

I wouldn't know what to say or who anyone was, plus you would need to mingle and then I would be all by myself."

"Slow down girl. I would never leave your side, wherever I go, you go, and the other reason I want you there is because you have made me so happy, I wanted to show everyone the reason for my happiness"

Frank really knew how to say the right words. I started to get emotional in the car and he knew it.

"Don't get upset. I'm glad that I've finally got you that's all, it was worth the wait and I would do it all over again if I had to." He put his hand on my knee as we continued our drive.

Rebecca called me not long after I arrived home and asked me if I had enjoyed the night out.

"Best time ever" I said making my mood a little lighter. She told me that Imogen tripped over and broke two toes hitting them on the side of the table. I started to laugh. "She's fun isn't she? You must definitely invite her out again"

"I will" and with that the gossiping continued for another forty, five minutes. I took out my laptop, something I had not been on for a while, to do some research on a project which was coming up at work. I checked my emails; again I had not done that since I came back from Miami and had two, hundred and sixty two in my inbox. Most were spam so I just deleted them.

Then I saw one from "rock chick" and knew it was from Isabelle. I went to delete it but curiosity got the better of me. It was dated the day after I had caught them together. My heart started to beat fast but I remained calm as I read it.

Hi Autum, I don't know what else to say to you except I'm sorry. I will not pretend that I have an excuse to do what I did because I don't. I was your best friend and I betrayed you in the worst possible way, but I will not take the blame alone. We have been seeing each other for months, and now that it's out in the open, I have no intention of giving him up, 'remember' I saw him first.

I could not fucking believe the cheek of that bitch, "I was your best friend; I want to make a go of it" then it dawned on me with the last statement, "I saw him first"

She had been after him all this time for the past three years behind my back and I was clueless. Did she do this as the ultimate revenge? The two faced cow.

Was it because he proposed to me that she decided enough was enough and used my damm working trip to make her move?

My blood started to boil as I continued to flick through my emails. There were another six from her which I deleted, although I looked at one which was on the last day I was in my apartment.

I cannot believe you got Jack beaten up because he broke off the engagement. *He broke up with me? Is that what he told the stupid bitch?"*

155

The only reason he did not press charges was because I pleaded for him not to. *Is this bitch for real?*

I now you're upset but you'll get over it, I really want to give this a go but you need to back off, you had your time and you blew it.

I blew it, well all I can say is what goes around comes around, he's all yours bitch, blinded by a fuck eh!!

I started to pace the bedroom floor, furious at how I was the villain in all of this. I started to type but then stopped myself, *history*. If she was that stupid to fall for his lies then they both deserved each other. Good riddance to bad rubbish, I told myself and shut down my computer before joining Frank in his study.

Frank was behind his desk, phone on loud speaker and fingers frantically typing away on his machine. He looked up and motioned that he was on the phone, *who would have thought?*

I stared at him for a moment and he looked just ravenous. I started to walk towards the table, slipping off things as I approached. He looked up and then did a double take. He started to mix up his words as he spoke and I smiled.

He tried to shush me away but I continued towards him. Now I was only in my underwear.

I wrote on his notepad for him to keep talking as he looked at me quizzically, but I was in that sort of mood, playful and naughty. I needed to de-stress.

How long could he hold out? I give him five minutes max!

The man on the phone was discussing a possible merger of their companies. I licked his ear with my tongue.

They exchanged background knowledge and figures and arguments for and against the proposition etc.

I turn his chair around and play with myself in front of him, which makes him go quiet.

"Are you still there Frank"?

"Sorry yes still here"

He loosened his shirt collar, and I took off my bra and bent over him to feed him. He sounded like someone trying to eat and talk at the same time.

"Sorry Frank, you should have told me you were eating". I try to stifle a laugh as Frank said he was just taking a bite. He quickly bites my nipple before releasing it, and we both smiled.

Frank now seemed in the mood for my games and I liked it.

They continued to talk business as I undue his shirt and pull it out of his trousers; he slides down a little more in his chair.

I play with his nipples and his head goes back, Frank using all his will to stifle a moan, his cheeks starting to flush as he gripped the arm rest and I go down. I take off his belt then unbuttoned his trousers and pulled it down, surprised to find my friend was already there to greet me, as I put my hand around his semi hard cock. He loses control and a moan leaves him.

"Tom. We need to take a rain check, not feeling to well, struggling to concentrate right now". I looked up at him and waved my finger to say naughty, naughty. As I put him fully into my mouth he sighs and the phone line goes dead.

"Are you trying to kill me woman?"

"Thought you needed a little pick me up" He gently put his hands on top of my head as he continues to feed me, deep into my throat.

"Oh yeah" he said, as I continued to suck him hard and fast. I could feel his veins staining against its skin, the swelling in my mouth as it grew inside me; I pull back as I licked the tip and the juice starts to flow. I push it back inside and he didn't hold out for long, he tilts his head back then forward as he watches me suck him then comes inside my mouth, I felt the salty warmness going down my throat as I swallow, he continues to feed me, pumping everything he had until he had nothing left to give, his breathing erratic. I gave him one last suck before I released him.

It was now Monday and I was back at work after my great weekend with the girls and Frank. I met up with Rebecca for a quick hello and got down to work. I would be working away Thursday and Friday in Leeds and I had asked Rebecca's manager if she could help me. The initial answer was no, but as I pointed out how great an asset she was in Miami, it did not take her long to change her mind, as long as she produced a written report when she returned.

Frank was also working away but he would be gone for a week and was leaving tomorrow morning. That meant I would be alone for the first time since moving in with him in that big house.

I worked late that night getting all the preparation done which meant that nothing would catch me off guard at the last minute and I could relax until I left. By the time I got in it was nine at night and Rosetta had left my dinner for me. I joined Frank in the dining area and just curled up on the sofa. This was nice, my man waiting for me when I got home.

We went to bed at eleven but it was four a.m. when I was awoken by "Frank junior" giving me my goodbye present and then I was alone.

Chapter Fifteen

Too good to be true!

Frank had now been away for two days and had rung me quite often each day; it was like he was still at work and not miles away.

Rebecca also kept the phone calls coming. I was sure Frank had told her to make sure I was ok, which I was.

It only felt strange eating at home by myself and going to bed without my heat source next to me. I wanted an early night tonight as I would be setting off to catch the six, thirty morning train to Leeds. I settled into bed and fell asleep and started to dream.

It was dark; I wasn't sure where I was, only that I was cold and had nothing on my feet. I heard screaming and realised it was coming from a woman and I started to panic, I cried out to her but got no reply.

I tried to stretch out my hand to find a switch but my hands had been tied to something - a chair. The screaming got louder and louder and I could hear someone coming towards me. I felt a sharp pain across my face and realised then, that the screaming had come from me but still I couldn't see.

My head had been yanked back and it felt as if half my hair had gone with it.

Then she spoke, "Whore Bitch" I would recognise that voice any day.

"Let me go. Why am I here?"

"We told you to watch your back but you wouldn't listen.

I felt someone pull something from behind my head and realised that I had been blindfolded. After a few blinks I focused and saw them both, Jack and Isabelle laughing at me.

I jumped out of bed sweating, panic sweeping through me. I thought I had put these bad dreams behind me; it was just too good to be true.

The same type of dream kept coming back to me, and that's what scared me. Could they be planning something? And if so, what would they get out of it besides seeing me shit scared, because right now it was working.

It was nearly five in the morning, so I decided to get up and have a shower, hoping that my day couldn't get any worse.

Rebecca met me on the platform and I told her of my night. "Why didn't you phone me?"

"It was late and it was nearly time to meet you anyway, I'm fine just struggling to see why I'm getting them again that's all"

"Something must be triggering it, have you been thinking about them lately?"

"God no" The only reason I can think of is that Isabelle has been sending me emails and like a fool I have been reading them.

And before you say anything, yes it was a silly thing to do and I did delete some of them"

"How many were there?"

"Seven. But I skipped most of them; this one just drew my attention"

The train had now pulled up and we took our pre-booked seats and popped our magazines on the table for reading later.

"What was so special about the one that drew your attention?"

"It was the day Jack tried to rap…" I stopped short of saying the word, as I remembered she didn't know.

"I hope to god you weren't just about to say what I think you said". I held my head down which confirmed what she thought. It was too dammed early in the morning to have this sort of conversation but I knew Rebecca would not let it drop and deep down I still owed her a lot so I told her what happened after I left work on that day.

"Why didn't you tell me?"

"It was bad enough Frank finding me in that uncompromising position. He asked me to call you but I couldn't, didn't want anyone else to know, I felt ashamed, scarred that you may have judged me"

"Judge you? Is that what you thought I would do?"

"At that time yes, I blamed myself for letting him in"

"But you said he forced his way in?"

"He did, but I still blame myself for not checking who it was before I opened the door". Rebecca held my hand over the table and no more words were said.

The trolley service came shortly afterwards and I ordered a large latte with extra sugar and a bacon sandwich. Rebecca had a drinking chocolate with a sausage and egg sandwich and we ate while looking at our magazines and talking about the latest gossip from them. After that, the journey went quickly.

We headed straight for our meeting and I had time for a quick de-brief with Rebecca before we headed into the room. This was my plan originally on the train but other things took over.

This meeting was over two days and today's meeting would be mainly introductions, going through why we were there, what our roles and responsibilities would all be and an overview of what could be done to sort out the failing company etc..

I left most of this ground work to Rebecca; I underestimated her abilities and only saw her true potential at times like this.

We broke for lunch and I took that time to apologise again to Rebecca for not telling her.

"I can't begin to know what you went through. It was bad enough seeing what he did to you the first time around, but then this, well it doesn't bear thinking about. Don't be afraid to tell me anything, I'm not in any position to judge you ok, just remember what I have said."

"I will" and with that we continued with our lunch. I was now missing Frank badly and needed him near me. We were both working so I didn't want to send him a text or to ring him, I would just have to wait until he contacted me first.

We closed the meeting at three, thirty and headed towards our hotel to check in. We were both on the same floor but only a few doors away.

My room was a double, with the standard fixtures and fittings; I tested out the bed as I now like them high thanks to Frank. I grabbed a quick shower and checked my phone. There were two missed calls from Frank so I called him back.

That's what I missed today, his voice, he was so upbeat I was glad his meeting was going well. I gave him an update about mine and told him that I would be meeting Rebecca for dinner at seven.

"I miss you Frank, really miss you."

"Is everything ok?"

"Fine" I said, "just miss you that's all, the bed is too big without you."

He laughs. "Be home soon" and then he said the words I'd been dreading.

"I love you."

I paused for a moment then said it right back without even thinking. "I love you too". I was shocked at the quickness with which I said it, but then I realised it didn't make me feel awkward, it just felt right. My heart was truly missing him and it made me feel like a love sick puppy.

Frank was in Milan, meeting up with some of his old contacts he had made over the years. You could say it was more of a social than business trip.

When he was in his hotel bedroom he lay back on the bed and was thinking about the last few months.

He thought how lucky he had been to finally get the woman he had always dreamt of, even though at the beginning he felt like it was only ever going to be a dream.

He thought back to that dreadful day he delayed going to her apartment when she met up with Jack and he knew that day would haunt him for a long time to come. How when he got there, the door was ajar and he could hear her screams, the way he saw her tied up like an animal about to be butchered and the way he had been fucking her, it made his stomach churn.

How could she have been so naive? How could I have been so stupid?

This was the man who she was about to marry, the man who would have given her children some day, but was also quite happy to rape her, the words sticking in his throat.

Every time he had been there for her and it had paid off, but just not this time. He wondered how badly it may have gotten if he did not pass by at all, how far Jack would have taken things, what damage he could have done to his precious Autum, images popping into his head that he shook away quickly, to sick to be given the time of day.

He remembers starring at her without her knowing and how beautiful she looked and he wanted to pinch himself at how lucky he had been. He worshipped the ground she walked on and would always be by her side.

She fulfilled all of his sexual needs and more, the way her naughty side came out when he wasn't or didn't expect it, and he loved her for that.

He wanted to show her off to the world and let them know she was his, and he planned to do so, but first, he wanted to plan a trip to see his parents and introduce her as his "future wife." Even the words felt right.

He noticed she sounded shocked when she heard him say that he loved her, but he truly did. These were his feelings and he hoped she didn't think he wanted her to say something that she thought she had to say back for his benefit.

He smiled as he thought about her beautiful face and the places she had explored with his body, which now starts to jerk in response, he remembered how she had taken him in her mouth, especially that day in his study when he tried his dammed hardest to remain professional until she consumed him altogether, sucking the life out of him.

No other woman could have done that to him, and no other woman would.

She brought out his desires before he got a chance to show them to her. She could read him like a book.

He relaxed as he pictured their last morning together before he left, the way he woke her up, his face between her legs and her soft moans that greeted him.

How she asked him to fuck her so much, that every time her pussy throbbed, she would think of him while she was away. He laughs out loud.

She was an explorer, always doing something out of the ordinary, never shy, getting a kick from the thrill, and he was only too happy to oblige. This was what she did to him and he never wanted it to end.

By now he was hard as hell and the only way he could stop himself from self pleasuring was to take a shower, which he did, and to refocus on his work.

I met up with Rebecca and told her that Frank had said he loved me.

"What did you say back?"

"I told him that I loved him too and I meant it. I never thought I would say that so soon but it's different with Frank, it's hard to put it into words"

"I can see it when you're together" she said. I thanked her and we ordered our food.

By now it was another late one and I dreaded the thought of a more dreams but I focused on Frank's words and drifted off to a peaceful sleep.

It was Friday and I was buzzing from a good night's rest. Maybe Rebecca was right, I must have been triggering these thoughts by focusing on something that they had done or said to me. I would think on that for future nights to come.

We sailed through the meeting and left at two, forty five to catch our three, sixteen train from Leeds.

The train, as always, was on time, and we sailed back home in no time. Once there, we caught the taxi to Rebecca's apartment then to mine.

Rosetta greeted me at the door and I smelt her lovely cooking again. She had cooked lamb shank, mashed potatoes and asparagus, with a side salad. What a welcome.

Chapter Sixteen

Being held against one's will is no laughing matter?

Frank was finally home and I missed him like crazy. He was hardly through the doors before we went to our room to have some sexy time together.

I also had some other good news to tell him, my apartment had been sold for the full asking price. Frank was over the moon and asked me what I was going to do with the money, but I had no plans yet. I was thinking of booking a surprise trip to the Bahamas so that he could visit his parents but this was still just an idea.

The charity ball was now only a week away but I was happy that I had my gown. It was an Aqua Blue satin dress which swept the floor. It swung across one shoulder and was fitted at the waist. The shoes and bag were also of the same material and I accompanied these with a simple chocker and matching bracelet.

Frank had his usual Black Tie attire which he would not show me until the event. How hard would it be to picture this outfit? But I still humoured him.

We popped into the solicitors to sign all the paperwork after work, and I felt that this was the only thing left in my old life that tied me to Jack and bad memories, but no more.

I thought that whoever had bought my apartment would love it as I used to and be happy there. Once all that was done we decided to go for a drive and stopped off at some village pub for a meal, a quick call was made to tell Rosetta not to cook tonight and then we were off.

Frank talked about the contacts he had made when he was abroad and how useful they had become, he mentioned that the business was really booming and that he may need to expand some areas of his workforce to meet demand, this was good news and I was really pleased for him, he had worked hard and it was now paying off.

As the evening drew to a close, I looked back on my life over the past few months and realised I had been on a roller coaster ride, but had survived it.

Rebecca had been praised by her manager for the report she had produced after our last business trip and was now in line for a bonus. I congratulated her as she more than deserved it.

We had planned to celebrate on the town again but this would be after my up and coming event with Frank, as we planned to make it a double celebration with the sale of my apartment.

On Thursday I went out for lunch with Rebecca to our favourite sandwich shop. I'd not been back there since meeting whore bitch and missed my favourite food. We left work at a different time for lunch, so I was confident that I would not meet her today, but I was never that lucky.

She was already inside being all loved up with Jack and when I thought I would get that pang or that sick feeling, I felt nothing when I saw them both together; in fact I totally bypassed them without a second glance and headed straight to the counter.

"You ok?" said Rebecca.

"Never felt better" I replied, and it was true.

As I was heading out of the shop I heard her say quite loud to Jack "I cannot believe you bought her flat"

I stopped and turned around as he replied "well, it held fond memories and is in a great location. If she was foolish enough to include fixtures and fittings, I'd be a fool not to go for it. The estate agent said he had loads of enquiries but I was a first time buyer with no chain, but the best part of it was when I told him that I caught my fiancé in bed with another woman I knew it was mine". They both started to laugh and I ran out of the shop.

"How could he do this to me? Why would he want to live there with that bitch?"

"Don't think about it now, they're just trying to wind you up"

I left the sandwich shop with food the furthest thing from my mind and headed back to work. I rang Frank to tell him who my new buyer was. The thought of having his money made this bitter sweet.

"You should squander some of his money, buy yourself a new car, remember two can play that game", and he was right, Jack was trying to get to me and all I wanted to do was to move on, but he always seemed to be there, always one step ahead.

Before I knew it, the charity dinner was here. Frank slipped into his Black Tie attire and looked sexier than

169

the pictures in his office. On slipping into my dress, I felt a million dollars and hoped Frank would think the same.

The dress was better than I had remembered when I tried it on. It hugged me in places I didn't realise I had.

Frank helped put on my choker, and then placed kisses down my neck.

"Frank, don't we need to get a move on?"

"We have plenty of time before we have to leave, we could…"

"Do you know how long it took me to get into this dress?"

"No, but I can tell you how quick I can get you out of it". He placed his hand on my bum and softly moved his hands up and down. "Frank" He pulled me in front of him. I could feel him getting aroused and said "down boy" before I smacked his arm and moved away.

I stood in front of the mirror to look at myself and even I gasped at my transformation. I decided to have my hair done at the hairdressers, wanting to look the perfect partner for Frank and looking at myself now, I couldn't argue.

"Ready?" he said as I grabbed my bag and headed downstairs to the limo he had hired for the event.

The hotel where the event took place boasted a grand glass entrance. There was a piano player to our right amongst the hoards of people in attendance and the waitress service was impeccable.

Not long after we arrived I met his friends from the golf range, David and Peter with their partners. We exchanged greetings and headed towards the main hall.

Our table was near the front of the stage but the room held around one, thousand people; Frank looked comfortable and spent most of the time nodding to people that he knew. This was a five course dinner so I needed to pace myself with the food and especially the drink which came in abundance.

Frank had prepared a small speech about the charity and the good causes the money generated from this evening's event would bring. He talked about a visit to a homeless shelter and how he had felt sleeping in a small room that housed eight in total, no private space with literally just the clothes on your back. How he went and spent the day out on the streets with a man called Steve and how he watched him rummaging through bins outside of food shops on the off chance that someone had thrown away their half eaten food, or left some of their drink and how Steve asked him to then go through the bins to see what he could find, Frank talks about how he had felt actually sleeping rough for one night and how his back ached the next day, the crowd laugh as Frank holds his back.

'Frank's talk lasted around forty, five minutes and it was heart wrenching. We know that there are people out there far worse than ourselves; sometimes it takes a speech like this to bring the message home, but will it make us change, and appreciate the things we have? I think we all know the answer to that.

Frank headed back to our table with pats on the back and "well said" together with standing ovations. I stood to give him a kiss as he sat down.

"That was lovely" I said as we continued with the arrival of tea and coffee.

The auction followed soon after, with mad biddings for weekend trips, spa breaks, experience days, luxury hampers, the list went on and on and so did the bids.

I needed some fresh air as all this body heat was getting too much. I excused myself from the table and told Frank I wouldn't be long. "Do you need some company?" No thank you, I won't be long, take this time out to mingle"

The air was fresh and the stars were shining bright. I took a deep breath and looked at the other people around me, some outside to smoke, others just to chat.

My phone started to ring and the caller ID was Rebecca. "Hi Rebecca what's up?"

"You need to come here now, he's here and he's asking for you"

"Who's there Rebecca? You're not making any sense"

"He said you must come here alone otherwise he's going to hurt me". She was sobbing.

I heard a scream as he took the phone.

"Your wasting time Autum, tick tock, tick tock". The phone line went dead.

Jack! My heart raced as I debated what to do. Rebecca had done so much for me and she needed me.

This was Frank's event and I could not ruin it for him either. I looked at my phone and looked back at the hotel as I left in a taxi, remembering that I told Frank I wouldn't be long.

I sent Frank a text message as I pulled up outside her building. I didn't want him to know that it had something to do with Jack as he would have left and I would have felt guilty.

Hi Frank, Rebecca's in trouble, will tell you more once I get there, and try not to worry, enjoy your evening, you deserve it.

Autum x

I pressed Rebecca's apartment number and she buzzed me in. I knocked on the door and my heart started pounding. She opened the door and I could see Jack behind her pulling at her hair, his right hand bending her arm behind her back, she must have been crying quite a lot as her mascara had run all the way down her face.

"Get in" he shouted before slamming the door behind me and locking it.

What the hell is he going to do now?

He stared at me for ages, looking me up and down before he said "sorry to interrupt your party but we have unfinished business you and I".

"Let her go Jack, we have no unfinished business we're over, you saw to that when you slept with that whore, now let us go before you get yourself into trouble"

"I'm the one talking bitch so shut the fuck up and listen"

I did as he said as he dragged Rebecca into her living room by the hair, still crying.

"Isn't this cosy"

"What do you want Jack, this needs to end now"

"Oh it will baby, just you wait and see"

The last statement threw me and I was scared that he was planning to do something stupid like kill us both, double suicide. My mind was racing and I couldn't focus.

I remained standing when he pushed Rebecca towards me, screaming as she hugged me.

"Sshhh it will be ok, sorry you got dragged into this, this is my mess."

"I'm sorry Autum; he cornered me as I was entering my apartment."

"You have nothing to be sorry about, just need to figure out what he's up to"

Jack leaves the room and comes back a minute later with drinks.

"Drink" I looked at Rebecca who then looked at me, *what had he put in it?*

"Do you want me to shove it down your throat? Drink" he shouted.

I took the glass first. This was about me and I wanted to protect Rebecca as best as I could.

"If anything happens to me, tell Frank I love him."

With that Jack charges at me and slaps me across my face sending me flying half way across the room in my tight dress, my hair had partly fallen down with the force of that hit, but he had also split my lip as I taste the blood in the corner of my mouth, and saw the contents of my drink on my dress where it had spilled.

Rebecca started to scream, but I had to compose myself for both of us when he left the room, only coming back to top up my drink. I knocked back the contents of the glass without hesitation. *It's whiskey.*

I felt nothing beside the warmness of the drink going down my throat. I tried to see if I could taste anything else but couldn't

Rebecca was still sobbing, as she held the glass to her mouth and swallowed.

"Now that wasn't hard was it ladies" he said as he started to laugh.

We both sat on the sofa as Jack paced up and down looking at his watch. *Is he expecting someone, Frank, or Isabelle maybe? Did he know that I would tell Frank where I was?*

I had been at the apartment for ten minutes now when Rebecca collapsed on my lap. I jumped, not knowing when it was going to be my turn. "Rebecca" I shouted, "She'll be ok, she should wake up in around, say three hours, now get up"

He grabbed me by the hand leaving Rebecca to slide off my lap and collapse on the sofa. He'd drugged her.

"Where are you taking me?"

"I'm taking you home"

Frank was having such a good time that he had presumed Autum was mingling with the other guests and his friends' partners; an hour had passed by since he had last seen her.

He was happy that his companions and associates had commented on how beautiful Autum was and how she should make an honest man out of him, he smiled at the recollection.

This was just more confirmation that he should propose as planned when they got home this evening.

In Milan he had bought a platinum diamond ring; this was not his intention when he saw it in the shop, but he was drawn to it. When he placed the ring in the palm of his hand, he knew it was meant for her.

David and Peter found Frank to say their goodbyes, but it was only then he realised Autum had not been seen since she went to get some air.

Frank decided to check his phone when he saw the text message. Panic rose as he knew that Rebecca had never been in trouble and that something was amiss. He rang straight afterwards and it went to voicemail; now he was really panicking.

The limo was beside him soon afterwards heading for Rebecca's. Frank kept trying to phone both Rebecca and Autum, but it went to voicemail; he didn't leave a message.

The limo parked outside Rebecca's and Frank darted to the building pressing all of the buttons until someone had let him in, Frank was soon banging on Rebecca's door but there was no reply.

After a few minutes he decided that there was no alternative but to try and kick down the door.

Neighbours came out asking what the hell was going on. Frank said that he thought something had happened to Rebecca after receiving a text and he needed to make sure both her and his fiancé was ok.

He listened to himself say the words fiancé and nearly wept; he wasn't going to lose her no matter what. Some neighbours then help kicked down the door until eventually it gave way.

He rushed in without thinking to be cautious, along with some of the neighbours. It was then that his heart sank as he saw Rebecca's lifeless body on the sofa.

"Call an ambulance" he shouted as they rushed out to do so. He was slapping her face but her whole body just kept flopping as he tried to hold her up.

"Rebecca wake up please, where's Autum?" but no response.

He laid her gently down and searched the apartment, quickly realising that it was empty. It was then he decided enough was enough and called the police.

The hospital confirmed that she had possibly been drugged or had taken some drug. Frank insisted that it was not in her character and that there were three

176

glasses in the room all with different drinks in them; he could tell by the smell.

It was now two hours since Autum had been missing and Frank needed Rebecca to wake up fast. He gave the police a description of Autum and Jack and what had happened leading up today, but it was hearsay and it wasn't enough for them to act. They also said it was too early to class her as a missing person.

Frank was furious. He knew he needed to keep a straight head, but it was too much, holding his hands over his face he sat down beside Rebecca on the chair and started to cry.

Not long afterwards Rebecca started to mumble and stir and Frank shot out of the chair as if the gun had gone off for the start of the race, Frank started to shake Rebecca's shoulders firmer than he had expected.

"Rebecca where's Autum?"

"Autum" she mumbled, eyes not fully open.

"Yes Autum, she came to meet you, is she with Jack?"

She mumbled her name again and Frank realised she would be of no help for another thirty to forty minutes.

"Can't you speed up her recovery?"

"She needs to rest, please give her some space" and with that he was ushered out of the room.

Pacing up and down, all he could think of was the scene that had greeted him when he went round to her apartment. He felt bad about the dreams she had described to him but had dismissed them as just that, bad dreams why did he not listen to her.

He was racked with grief and guilt that he had not sorted Jack out sooner and now he would pay the ultimate price.

Jack was evil and wanted to punish Autum that he knew. He needed to think of any place that he could have taken her, but couldn't; it was not something that ever came up under the circumstances.

He heard screaming and ran back into the room to find Rebecca confused by her surroundings. "Frank"

"Oh dear god Rebecca where is she?"

"He took her I'm sorry, he drugged me."

"Do you remember anything that was said before you passed out?"

She was thinking and thinking hard. I think, then she trailed off.

"Please Rebecca; I cannot lose her, not now"

"She did say to tell you that if anything happened to her that she loved you"

Frank broke down; it was too much for him to take in.

"I think I heard him say that he was taking her home, but I'm not sure if I just imaged that before I passed out"

"Home? What does that mean?"

Frank thought of their home but dismissed it. She would never take him there and he knew he did not know where he lived either, but to be sure he rang, and when Rosetta answered the phone he felt relieved.

It had now been nearly three hours and Frank still had no idea where she could be, until Rebecca remembered that conversation in the sandwich shop.

"I know this may sound silly but if he did say that, there is only one place I can think of".

"Where?"

"He's bought her flat remember, he's taken her back to her flat"

Frank's world went black.

178

Chapter Seventeen

Too weak to talk, too much pain to touch.

Autum had also been drugged but it took longer for her's to kick in; she remembered part of the journey back to her apartment but nothing more.

Her dreams started coming to life in her head but this time they were real and she knew that if she opened her eyes it would still be there waiting for her.

She felt herself stirring out of her sleepy state, her mouth dry as she tried to lick her lips, the sharp sting in the corner of her mouth, a reminder of what Jack had done.

"Wakey, wakey sleepy head?"

She tried to focus on where the voice was coming from but was still drowsy; she tried to lift up her head but she felt it flop back down again. Something strong was now under her nose and she started to cough as she inhaled it. She looked to see familiar surroundings and felt bile rising into her mouth; she was on her back and felt like she was choking.

She tried to automatically cover her mouth but couldn't move. She looked around to find he had tied not only her hands but her feet as well.

She was still weak but asked him "why?"

"Because I love you, and because I know deep down that you love me too" *denial.*

"I did but I don't anymore" I tried to struggle but the bonds didn't budge.

"I will make you love me again Autum, it will be better than last time I won't ever hurt you again."

"Let me go Jack, please"

She felt cold and realised that she was naked, on the bed, her hands and legs apart; she looked around and saw that her beautiful dress had been cut up. *Bastard.*

"You won't get away with this Jack; it's called kidnapping and rape"

Jack tried to give me some more drink and I sealed my mouth shut as he tried to pry it open. He then pinched my nose so that I could not breathe and when I went to take a breath he poured it down. I spat some out into his face, but knew that some had gone down as I coughed; he wiped his face then started to strip as I wept. *No Frank to save me this time.*

He was already hard as he climbed on the bed, trying to fondle my breasts as I tried to buck him off but he just put more of his pressure on me.

"You used to like this" I didn't reply.

I turned my head in shame, refusing to give him the satisfaction.

At this moment in time, my body went numb at this intrusion, this wasn't Frank it was some sicko who was trying to have something that didn't belong to him anymore, a bastard that thought he could have his cake and eat it.

I scream "shouldn't you be doing this with your bitch" and I spat at him again" Jack slaps me but I felt hardened to the pain.

"Oh once I finish with you, I will make sure that when I fuck her, your face will be what I see when I come"

I tried to buck him off again and he slaps me even harder in my face; boy, that pain really hurt, but I found that it kept me alert. I decided that if that's was what it takes for me to stay awake then pain it would have to be.

Jack starts to stoke me with his cock in-between my legs as I tried in vain to close them.

He groaned

"You sick bastard." I felt a little sleepy now and panicked, *keep awake!*

I needed a plan but had limited time to think. Jack liked to have sex, so this would be the only way I could trick him, and if it didn't work, he would punish me far worse than he had already, but it was worth the gamble.

"Put it in my mouth Jack, let me suck you"

He stopped for a minute and looked at me and I did not know what he was thinking, I began to moan and lick my lips and rose up my hips to grind him.

He moaned again then stopped. "Do you think I'm that stupid? What, you expect me to put it in so that you can what? Bite it off?"

"Look Jack" I said in my most sleepy sexy voice, "you're right, I can never love anyone else but you, it will always be you, don't you want me to suck you, lick you, and make you come in my mouth?"

He thinks for a minute and I find his weak spot, *they always think with their dicks!*

"If you do anything stupid Autum, you'll regret it."

He slid further up and was now above me; bile was lurking at the back of my throat as I contemplated what I was about to do, but in my mind, this was the better of two evils when it came to Jack. I would not let him penetrate me and would do whatever I had to.

181

I opened my mouth for him and he hesitated before slowly putting in it then drawing it quickly back out, testing the waters.

"I need you Jack" and like a fool he put it back in. I teased him with my tongue and he slid it in deeper. I looked up at this man with hate as I continued to suck him; I choked when he went in too deep. When he pulled it out, I told him that I was no threat and that he should at least untie me. I told him that I knew he had drugged me again and that I was already feeling sleepy so he had nothing to lose.

"Let me enjoy this with you properly before I sleep" I said before pretending to roll my eyes and let my head loll back, as if the drug had started to kick in. He untied me quickly. *Ruled by the promise of a fuck?*

"Let me fuck you?" he said.

"Not yet let me play with you first?"

I kissed him over his shoulder as I looked around the room for an object of some sort, nothing. I kissed him again quickly as I looked again before spotting the scissors by my dress.

"I'm sorry for leaving you" I said. "Can you ever forgive me?"

"You know I can? That's why I bought your flat, I knew we would be together again and wanted you to have somewhere to live?"

He really was deranged!

By this time my head really was swaying and not because of me. I swung him onto his back and straddled him.

"You're so sexy from here" he said.

"And you'll be soon dead" I said to myself.

My time was running out and I was losing control fast. I slid down and put his cock back in my mouth until he was moaning and his eyes were closed. I tried to reach for my dress but it was still too far.

I stopped to say I needed the toilet which drew suspicion, but I told him that I was more than happy for him to follow me, which he did.

I dabbed cold water on my face and returned with him back to *that* room. I told him to sit at the edge of the bed; he did so like a lap dog.

I started to dance for him picking up my torn dress but managing to swoop up the scissors at the same time. My back was towards him and I bent over fully so that his mind was on other things, my ass hovering over his face. I turned quickly around and lost my balance, he grabbed me to steady me. My vision was going, and going fast.

I flung him back onto the bed telling him that the dance could come later and put the dress where I could reach it.

Again I pretended to moan as I made him touch me, every movement making my stomach churn. As I stroked him back his breathing had now picked up speed and his mind was lost to his up and coming orgasm *or death.*

"Harder" he said, as I increased my hold around his cock and the speed that I was doing it.

I changed over hands as I reached for the scissors, hate consuming my every stroke and every suck I gave him. I looked at my hands and feet and saw the red lines, a reminder of what Jack had done to me in the name of love; I looked up at him and the fact that he felt no shame at what he was doing to me as long as he got his kicks, he then interrupts my thoughts as he cries out and gripped the sheets before he closes his eyes.

This was it, my only chance; I grab the scissors and plunged it into his chest, prompting him to scream out with pain.

"You bitch; I'm going to kill you" but before he could react, I knocked his head back with my fist, feeling now that I had broken something the noise of bone cracking, this really woke me up.

I quickly grabbed the rope and turned him over, he screams, as the scissors go in deeper. I then grabbed his feet and tie them both together; I then wrap the rope around his hands so that he could not stand up and could only rock, my heart was now going ten to the dozen, helped by the adrenalin.

I could not see him now, my vision had gone, but I could here him cursing me and screaming at me just as his voice started to fade in my head unsure if this was real, this is before I collapsed; the room spinning was the last thing I remember, unsure of where I would end up.

Frank rushed out of the hospital and headed back home; if she was there he remembered that he still had the spare key to her apartment never thought of handing it into the estate agents.

He tried to get help from the police but they told him there was nothing that they could do. He would die for this woman because she meant everything to him and without her in his life, there would be no life.

Frank wasn't a fighter but knew that he would do whatever it took to make sure she was ok, and with that he left in his own car and drove like a maniac.

How would he find her? Would she be hurt? What if she wasn't there?

He couldn't think of any other alternative but prayed that this hunch paid off and that indeed the sick bastard had taken her back to her own apartment.

Diving out of his car, he fumbled with the keys, nerves and anxiety kicking in. When he reached the door he stopped, his breathing too loud and heavy for his liking, his heart beating heavy against his chest, he leaned in towards the door and listened.

He heard no noise so quietly let himself in.

He could smell her perfume and his heart sank, but he still couldn't hear anything and that disturbed him.

Looking into the living room he saw nothing only her purse. He knew there was no one in the kitchen as he could see it from where he was.

"The bedroom?" This was one room Frank was dreading the most; he pictured the same scene that greeted him before, but he could not hear no noise, no screaming no muffled noises, nothing!

He pushed open the door and first saw Jack lying on his stomach all tied up with blood on the sheets. Jesus!

Then he saw Autum, naked and lying lifeless on the floor. He rushed over to her and tried to feel for a pulse, it was there but it felt weak. He pulled out his phone and called for an ambulance and the police and waited until they turned up.

Frank covered parts of her body with his jacket, sparing the scene that would greet the emergency services when they arrived.

He could only imagine what Autum had gone through and what she did to survive, and at this moment in time he was mad as hell at her for not letting him leave the function, but proud of what she had done all by herself, but at what price had she paid for it.

The police and ambulance had arrived together. Frank told them that he thought she may have been drugged but was unsure, and that they both had a pulse so he also knew *he* was still alive.

Jack then jumped out of what could only be described as delayed shock and started to scream as the medics started to undue his ropes so that they could get a better look at his injuries.

"That bitch tried to kill me" he gasped.

Frank lunged at him and hit him straight on the jaw before being pulled back.

The police were now taking notice of what Frank had been trying to tell them earlier. They now wanted him to make another statement, but he just ignored them and followed Autum into the ambulance.

Chapter Eighteen

What goes around comes around.

At the hospital I was still undergoing some tests to make sure that I was ok and no other symptoms were found.

Frank popped in to see Rebecca but she had already discharged herself.

When I came round my first words were "sorry"... Frank held my hand and kissed my forehead before telling me that it was over.

"Is he dead?"

"No, just a surface wound, he'll live but the police will be talking to him later."

"Is he here?" He paused before he said "yes"

I was in too much pain, my face and body hurt and my emotions as well as the drug wearing off was taking its toll. Talking of the police, they came in not long afterwards and as I was well enough to talk to them I told them everything from the start.

"Are you going to arrest me?"

"No, but we may need to talk to you again if that's ok"

I said "thanks" and they left.

I looked at Frank and he joked "we should stop meeting like this" and I gave a dry laugh.

It took me a while before I remembered Rebecca, "Oh god is Rebecca ok?"

"She's fine, discharged herself already"

"Please Frank, will you ring her and tell her how sorry I am, please?"

"I will now rest for a short while"

Frank left the room as he took out his phone. I thought to myself, could this really be over, will my dreams finally come to an end? I just wasn't sure, I just wasn't that lucky.

Thinking of Frank finding me yet again in a state of nakedness, all I could do was laugh to myself. How much more could he take? How much baggage can one person handle? And that's how I felt, Frank taking on baggage and did he think I was worth it.

I sat up in bed waiting for his return and then heard someone crying, the noise coming in and out of my eardrums sporadically. It was a voice I could not seem to get rid of:

Whore Bitch?

I swung my painful body out of the bed to follow the noise; why would she be crying? Did that mean he was dead? Was Frank lying to me?

The noise got louder as I approached a drawn curtain. What am I doing here? I hope he rots in hell. But still I needed to see him and her to close this chapter for good.

I drew back the curtain and she was sitting on the chair, her body hanging over the bed and her hands holding him tight. She looked up at me with vengeance but did not say a word at first.

"You tried to kill him?" I looked at Jack with a dressing slung across his chest where I had stabbed him, *obviously not deep enough.*

He was awake and staring back at me but not saying a word.

"He raped me, twice Isabelle, your precious loving boyfriend?" The man I was engaged too...

"What do you mean raped you?" she said confused.

She looked at Jack then back at me and started to laugh.

"Liar" she shouted, "you went round for one last fling, when he refused you, you tied him up and then stabbed him, cut up your clothes and cried rape"

I took in the scene in front of me and thought only one thing. *Fool.*

I looked at Jack, who by then had turned his head to the side, too ashamed to face me the spineless bastard.

"You claim you love me Jack, so for once in your life, tell the fucking truth" and with that I walked off.

Frank had of course returned and was frantic when he did not see me.

"You can't just get up and walk away, you should be resting, where did you go?"

"I went to see him"

"Jesus Christ Autum, what the bloody hell for?"

"Just wanted him to do the right thing for once, that's all, I didn't stay, just said my piece and left them to it"

"Them?"

"Yes, the bitch is here too"

He gave me a hug and then tucked me back into bed.

"I want to go home" I said.

189

"But you may be suffering from shock?"

"Please Frank, do whatever it takes, just take me home, now"

"Ok, I'll see what I can do, but stay in that bloody bed" and with that he left.

Frank came back with a consultant who looked at my charts, as they do and was happy that I had responded well, to what, I wasn't sure, but he said that I could leave and that I needed, well you guessed it, plenty of rest.

I was in a hospital gown with my ass was sticking out at the back, no matter how you hold them; the string seems to always be missing where you need it most.

"Did you get hold of Rebecca?"

"Yes, she is still shaken by her ordeal and will be staying with her family for a while, I told her to take as much time off as she needed I will clear it with work"

"Has she said anything about me?"

"Only that she's glad that you're ok and that you are very lucky to have someone who loves you like I do".

I looked at Frank, tying to see if he added that last bit in himself, he was gauging my reaction, I could tell.

"I do love you Frank, I really do"

We kissed for a while, the pain in my face a hurtful reminder; he put his jacket over me as we headed out of the room.

We had gotten less than fifty yards when I was greeted by the bitch with a hot drink in her hand. My main concern at first was that she would throw it at me and Frank thought the same and stood in front of me as protection.

"He's told me everything" she said sobbing as she spoke. I peeped over Franks shoulder.

"Everything?" I said.

"Yes, everything"

I now side stepped Frank and walked towards her.

"And you still want him?" I said shocked at what she had told me.

"I love him; I wanted him from the beginning before you took him away from me"

"He didn't want you, and I did not take him away from you," I paused for a moment but then said, "can I ask you something" I added.

"What?" she replied?

"Was this your plan all along to take Jack away from me?" There was no reply and with that I slapped her, well for that split second I did only intend to slap her but then my fist formed so I used that instead. It may have been the release I needed and it felt good, she fell back and her tea spilled over her hand and on the floor, as she clutched her face crying I said to her that I was glad it happened, if not for any other reason that *you* bought me and Frank together, you both deserve each other and what goes around, comes around. "Come on Frank," and with that we walked away.

On arriving home Frank treated me as if I had just given birth. I was fine except for the odd tingle in my face and the odd headache, but Frank was having none of it as he tucked me in.

"Frank?"

"The doctor said rest and if I have to pin you down myself" he stopped, realising what he had said and apologised.

I just burst out laughing. "Don't feel you have to watch what you say, I'm fine really"

He must have thought I was still recovering from shock. "You scared me today"

"And I'm sorry. I tried to do the right thing by both of you and I messed up"

"I would have dropped everything for you, you know that?"

"I do know" and with that he tucked me even tighter into bed.

Frank took the next two days off but I had to force him to go back into work after that. I reminded him that Rosetta was here so I would want for nothing, so he went in.

The phone calls kept coming on the hour from Frank so I texted him and told him to work!

He had placed an order of flowers to be delivered to where Rebecca was staying along with flowers to be delivered here.

I also had the chance to ring Rebecca myself on most days. I found I could not apologise enough for what I had put her through but she said "what's done is done" and that she had moved on and was looking forward to going back to work as she was bored, and that her family were feeding her to much "get well food" I laughed.

I talked about what I wanted to do as a "Thank You" to Frank for everything he had done for me and that with some of the money from the sale of the house I wanted to surprise him with a trip to see his parents in the Bahamas.

"Bahamas?" she screeched down the phone.

"Yes, he has not been over to see them and I thought what better way to get to meet them, plus get a tan at the same time, we both laugh. Do you think that may be too much?"

"He will love it"

I hung up the phone and thought more about the present I wanted to give him and made some initial enquires.

Frank needed to phone Autum as he would be working late, but he also wanted and make some plans to take a trip to the Bahamas to see his parents, *finally*.

He started to ring Autum often until she sent him the text that he was being over protective and that he needed to work, but he couldn't help himself. Frank picked up the phone and phoned his parents.

"Hi mom"

"Hi Frank, how are you?"

"Well thanks and dad?"

"He's ok, missing his son as always"

"That's why I was ringing you?"

"I'm confused? What do you mean?"

"I was planning to visit you in a couple of weeks and wanted to know if you could take some time off"

There was a pause on the phone.

"Mom, are you still there?"

"Yes dear", another pause. "Is everything ok? You're not ill are you?"

He laughs; "no mom, just wanted you both to meet someone"

The line went quiet again.

"A woman?"

This time he really laughs. "Of course mom"

She called Frank's dad and I could hear her saying quietly "Frank is coming over and wants us to meet someone"

"A woman?" he replied and Frank's mom said yes.

"Son, we're so happy for you, of course you can come, just confirm the dates and we will take the time out, anything for you son, you know that, just can't believe you will finally be coming over"

He handed mom back the phone.

"Son, she's not, you know"

"No she's not pregnant mom." Frank shook his head as he laughs to himself.

"Miss you son" she said. Frank paused, feeling guilty that it had taken him meeting someone for him to hop on a plane to see his parents.

"Miss you too mom" and with that he kissed the phone and told her he would see her soon.

Chapter Nineteen

You know they're up to something when they keep smiling.

I was now back at work after two reluctant weeks off. So much seemed to have changed and I had a lot of work to catch up on. At least the last time off was classed as holiday.

Rebecca was also back and lucky for me, our friendship did not suffer. I had slept so well over the past few weeks and I knew in my heart that my ordeal was over.

I was so happy with Frank and the amount of love and attention that he showed me. I told Rebecca that I had decided to book the trip for him to visit his parents but would do it nearer Christmas time and that would be my Christmas present to him, which was going to be four months away.

She also told me that she and Julian had become a lot closer over the last few weeks; he even came out to visit her when she was off. I was pleased for them both as Julian was a nice guy, she couldn't ask for more.

When Frank came home that evening he had the biggest smile on his face.

"You're happy?" I said, "Is there something I should know about?"

"Just had a good day at work, that's all" before he kissed me and swooped me up.

"Ok" I said, looking even more puzzled.

We ate and Frank still had that smile on his face. What was up with him?

He spent the next few hours in his study and I retired upstairs and checked my emails.

There were one hundred and twenty eight in total, but I took out the junk ones and names I didn't know. I sifted through what was left but there was nothing much in there.

He came up late as I was resting, and I felt him brush his nose by my ear and kiss me on my cheek. I turned to face him, breathing in his aftershave.

"Are you asleep?" I nodded my head, and wrapped my hands around his neck. He lifted me up and I wrapped my legs around him as we kissed.

My tongue was so deep inside his mouth I moaned as the pleasure built up inside of me, two weeks without this.

He placed me back on the bed and started to undress, but I stopped him, this was my job to undress *him* and I wanted to enjoy seeing every part of him bare.

I'd missed this over the weeks but he knew I wasn't ready; I tried to undo his shirt buttons slowly but Frank interjected and not far from ripped his shirt off, yanking at the cuffs, I smile.

I unzipped his trousers as he stepped out of them, his bulge plain to see and I looked back up at him.

"He missed you" and I laugh.

"Tell him I missed him too"

He lifted up my top and my excitement was also plain to see, my nipples already hard and waiting, the need to be sucked, licked, pinched and bitten, I wanted it all.

I pulled down his boxers and his cock bounced free. As I looked at it, it rose even more.

My bottoms followed shortly. He grabbed my breast and fitted as much of it in his mouth as possible. He bent down and widened my legs as if the world was coming to an end and this was his last fuck, but what a way to go, he buried his head there licking and sucking, just at the right level, soft but sensual as he dragged me down to the floor placing me on my back and lifting me high enough so that my bottom was off the floor and my legs were hanging over his shoulder, I go to take in a breath as Frank rams his cock into me.

"Ahh" as the pain hit me first and the pleasure took over soon afterwards. This was what I loved the most, the way he fucked me, hard and fast, his balls thrusting against me.

The noises Frank was making was pushing me even closer to climax, "more" I said as he pulls out of me and turns me over, I was now on all fours as he enters me from behind.

I meet his trusts by pushing back upon him, he gives my bottom a smack and I make a noise as the pleasure goes through me again.

His pace never slowed and I was sure I was going to get carpet burns at this rate, nothing a pair of trousers wouldn't hide I thought to myself.

We stopped again as we change positions Frank now lying on the floor as I straddled him, his cock shooting straight up my insides. I'm sure it was trying to find another way out.

We both moaned together, our bodies both hot and clammy; this was what sex should be like.

I rode him over and over, bouncing on him as he rammed his cock further in, his hips lifting off the floor as his hands gripped my waist pulling me down to meet his thrust.

The hardness took over as he swelled inside me, his breathing telling me that he was about to burst.

I squeezed my clit tighter as he grabbed hold of my ass and he came, shooting hot juice right in me over and over; I came not long after, my insides throbbing and sucking all that he had left inside to give me, before collapsing next to him on the floor.

We stayed like that for some time, with him still inside me, still semi hard as I rested my hand on his chest, waiting for his breathing to go back to normal.

We cleaned ourselves up and went to bed, but Frank was not sleepy at all so we talked.

"I've booked us a little break away, nothing fancy, we leave next Friday"

I shot up out of bed, "How long for?"

"Two weeks?"

"But I can't, I have a lot on at work, I can't replan that much in such a short space of time, plus I have not been back long, what must they think of me?"

"I've already cleared it"

"Don't tell me you have given it all to Rebecca?"

"Nope" I didn't know what else to say, he was smiling again and I had no clue why.

"Where are we going?"

"You'll know once we get to the airport" and with that he kissed me and said goodnight.

He was leaving me to stir and I knew that he was still smiling even though his back was towards me. I lay back down and thought of all the places that I would love to see, Barbados, Antigua, Turks & Caicos, the list went on but it had to be as a tourist and not via a business trip as you never truly can spend the time sightseeing, so could it be what this was, a business trip he was taking me on?

I gave up after a while and drifted off to sleep.

At work I told Rebecca about Frank's trip but she just kept saying don't forget to take lots of pictures if you get time and get some sexy bikinis and don't forget to buy sun block.

It was only then that I realised I didn't even know if we were going to Europe or further afield, so I planned to ask him tonight at home.

"Frank, this trip we're going on, would I need to take some sun block?"

"Whatever you think you may need dear" He was smiling again.

"Will it be hot?"

"I think they said the weather should be pleasant."

"Ahh Frank, just tell me, I need to plan."

This drama went on for days and I gave up in the end. He was being so cagy but I loved how he looked and how "this trip" was making him happy, he radiated and that made me love him even more.

It was time to pack and I tried to sneak a peak at what he was packing but he shooed me out every time. When he was in his study he would lock his case; he could hear me screaming as he shouted from downstairs.

"Knew you couldn't keep away"

I took Rebecca's advice and bought some new things for a beach holiday just in case. If it was too cold I could buy things once I was there. My sun block and hat were packed and before I knew it we were at the airport.

Frank took a call and I was shocked he was still talking shop, and that he had brought his phone along with him.

"I thought we were going to have a relaxing holiday?"

"We are, just making sure things are in order"

"Will you now tell me where we are going?"

He took me by my hand and told me to shut my eyes. This is hard when you're pulling a very heavy suitcase, but I did as I was told.

"Open". At first I felt silly as the first thing I took in was the people around me, and then I looked up, above the check in desk to see the destination.

"Bahamas"

"Were going to see your parents?"

"Yes I hope you don't mind, I suppose I shouldn't have sprung this on you but I wanted it to be a surprise"

"Glad I never booked my flight then"

"What do you mean?"

"I also wanted to surprise you, to say thanks for everything you have done for me and was going to surprise you at Christmastime to see them"

"You would do that for me?"

"I love you silly, it was the least I could do"

We travelled business class and the service was excellent. I've never travelled business class before and boy this really was in a class of its own.

The journey went by quickly and I was awake for most of it. I wanted to find out more about his parents before we got there. I forgot how nervous it could be meeting someone's parents for the first time as I knew first impressions count.

Our luggage came out quick and we headed through customs. I started getting jittery as I knew that they would be waiting on the other side of the doors.

He took my hand as we went through, "you're shaking?"

"Nerves", I said, "let's hope they like me"

"They will"

Chapter Twenty

Can men be romantic? of course they can.

"Frank, we're over here."

Frank looked around the crowd that had gathered waiting for friends, family and loved ones and he spotted his mother's beaming face followed by his dad.

We made our way towards them and Frank's mother greeted him with the biggest mothers hug and kisses, something Frank had not had in a long time, but then again, for his mom, it had been a long time.

She finally let him go and looked at Autum.

"Mom, dad this is Autum."

They looked at me for some time as my heart started to pound, then she grabbed me in a bear hug and said "we're so glad to meet you Autum." His dad then gives me a slight hug and a kiss on the cheek and I blushed.

"It's lovely meeting you too." I say back.

Frank's dad gave his son a man hug and a few pats on the back. "Nice to see you son"

"You to dad" and with that we headed towards the car park introductions over.

His mom was in her fifties with short blond hair and a fringe. She was elegantly dressed in a pink dress but no additional jewellery except her watch and kitten heels her English accent still coming out now and then as she spoke.

His dad was around the same height as Frank, with mousey hair, more casual than his wife in pants, a shirt and sandals and probably around the same age as his mom.

Our drive lasted around forty, five minutes and his mom was in full swing. She mentioned how hot it had been over the last few weeks and that we have picked a great time to come over, how well the business had been doing, and how close the beaches were to where they lived, she was bombarding us with information and sites as we made our journey to there home, it was only when Frank started to laugh that she said "too much?"

"It's fine mom" Frank said, as his dad shook his head.

We pulled up outside a large cream house with plenty of windows and balconies and little palm trees outside the front lawn. The house itself boasted five bedrooms and four point five bathrooms even though I never understood the point five. The dining hall curved around the house and then blended into another room with a ground floor bedroom with en-suite shower room just off it.

The kitchen was huge with white units, large American fridge and all the mod cons that you could need. She obviously loved this room you could tell.

Upstairs had a further four large bedrooms all en-suite.

"I hope this room will be ok for you both"

"It's lovely mom and thanks again." She left us to put our things away.

"See they're not that bad? And that was the easy bit"

"What do you mean?"

"Well you've got to get through a whole heap of food next" and I laughed. I changed into something more comfortable and we headed downstairs, Frank then heads off into another room with his dad and gives me a wink before he leaves.

"Do you need any help with anything?" I asked

"No dear, you're my guest have a seat and relax, would you like a drink? You must be thirsty?"

"Yes please anything will do".

"Ice tea?"

"Thank you."

I looked around lost for a bit but then his mom said "he talks very highly of you, he sounded so happy and I think you have something to do with that"

I smile, thinking of how he had spoken highly of me to his parents. His mom, or Elena as she liked to be called, mentioned a big family gathering on Saturday night and that she needed to do some more shopping. I could understand why she wanted to do it, her only son had come to visit with his girlfriend and she wanted to show us off, well maybe more him than me to her friends and relatives that lived in the area.

When Frank and his dad James came back in, they were both smiling, *what was going on with that smile?* He asked me if Elena had mentioned the up and coming gathering and I said yes, with Frank now by my side gently squeezing my waist.

The next few days went by quickly; we spent a day at the family business and then a day at the beach which was so close to the house you could walk there within five minutes.

By the time Saturday came around, I felt more than relaxed and part of the family. Frank was introduced to so many people, business of course entered some of the conversations and contacts were exchanged, he looked right at home. The laughter, food and drink were in abundance and the night ended around 4am in the morning, what a long day but it was great, Frank was so happy and felt at home.

Frank and James had been disappearing most days, golf I suppose as I know he also loved the sport, but I didn't mind as me and Elena was getting on great and swapping recipes as mothers do.

My skin looked golden brown and I looked healthier.

Elena took me into town to look at some clothes as another event was planned tomorrow, I don't know how they do all this socialising, it was wearing me out!

It was a beach front dinner which sounded nice so I wanted something to opt for a long and flowing cocktail dress as I pictured walking on the beach with Frank afterwards with no shoes and the warm breeze hitting our faces the sand between our toes.

"This is beautiful" Elena said. She had taken up a pricey cream laced dress, strapless, fitted at the waist then flowing to the floor.

"It is beautiful but don't you think that would be too much for a dinner?"

"Not at all, the venue is quite exclusive; the waiting list to get in can go back weeks and the dress code, well I'm sure you can image for that type of establishment.

"Oh," I said.

The dress was indeed beautiful but at $1,750, I wasn't sure I could justify the price.

"Try it on" she said, and I did. The dress was indeed perfect; the length just swept the floor but would be fine with heels I thought.

"You will be the belle of the ball in that" and I noticed she was getting emotional.

206

I took it off and put it back on the rail.

"Don't you like it?"

"I do, but it's a bit pricey."

"Nonsense, this is my gift to you."

"I couldn't, it's too much" I said, as she took it off the rail and headed to the counter.

"You shouldn't have, I will get Frank to reimburse you"

"I will have no such thing; it makes a change to be able to splash out on somebody other than myself" Elena laughed, and I smiled back.

Frank was in a flap as we started to get ready for the dinner. "What's up with you?"

"I need to pop out with my dad; he thinks he didn't put the alarm on at work and won't relax until he checks, so I said that I would go with him."

"Do you want us to wait until you get back; it shouldn't take you that long should it?"

"No, just head there and we will meet you". He kissed me, and then dashed out with the rest of his clothes in a suit carrier.

"Men," I collected my dress from my wardrobe forgetting that I didn't have a chance to show Frank. This heat was a killer and I was now happy with my choice or should I say with Elena's choice, as the dress would make me feel a lot cooler.

My hair was up as I wanted it off my neck, although I left a few strands coming down and wore no accessories.

Elena knocked on my room as I told her to enter, she gasped.

"Do I look ok?"

"Perfect."

"Are you ready?" she said, to which I nodded.

"Well, let's go" and with that we headed into our awaiting car and drove to the venue.

She wasn't wrong about the venue and by the look of the cars and the men waiting to relieve you of your keys while they park your car for you outside, I was now glad of the dress and hoped it was good enough for me to get in. The hotel door was opened for us and we were greeted inside Elena confirmed who we were.

"Wow, this really is posh." I say and Elena laughed.

"Nothing to good for my son and his girlfriend"

I looked around and still could not see Frank or his dad as signs of worry started to show on my face.

"Don't worry they will be here" Elena replies, we are still a little early.

A beach wedding must have been taking place.

The seats were already filled with people, all beautifully dressed in their outfits and hats and guest waving fans to keep them cool. I couldn't see the couple, but the setting was beautiful.

Along the beach leading to the alter, they had a white cloth sprinkled with red petals, each white chair had a sash with a bunch of flowers at the end of each bay.

The main alter displayed the most beautiful array of draping flowers, I was lost in my own dream when we were told that they were ready for us.

I knew we would be heading outside or near outside only because I was told it was a beach dinner. As we went through the double doors I realised that it was stupid of me to wear heals so I took them off. This part had to be unladylike and I apologised to Elena for not thinking properly about my footwear.

As we walked onto the warm sandy beach, Elena linked my arm in hers and kissed me. I realised the direction we were heading was towards this wedding party and I froze.

Elena opened up her purse and said "something old" before pulling out a blue sapphire bracelet and saying "you are already wearing something new."

I was speechless and could not take in what she had just said, but held out my hand, as if in a trance and she slipped it on.

Heads started to turn as I saw a figure coming towards me and it was my father, *how the hell did he get here?*

"Dad"

"You look radiant Autum" he said. I stuttered as I asked where mom was and he pointed towards the front.

"I had no idea dad believe me, I". He cut me off. "Frank told me weeks ago and I was only to happy to help" *how long had he been planning this?*

I looked towards the altar and saw a fetching young man looking back at me and then it hit me. My heart was pounding and I wanted to cry, a lump sticking in my throat.

As I walked what felt like the green mile I saw faces that I had never seen before and faces I had encountered recently at his parent's house not so long ago.

I heard sobs to my left and saw Rebecca and Julian. *I didn't even spot them. She got up to give me a bouquet. She was in on it too?*

I walked in a daze as I headed near the front and my mother stood up to greet me with a kiss and a hanky.

"You look beautiful."

"Thanks mom."

I heard a song playing and I started to cry, it was "Unforgettable" by Nat King Cole.

My dad took over from Elena and started to pat my arm as we headed towards the altar and still I couldn't talk. Frank then turned around; he was in a cream suit, his top buttons undone and no shoes, I tried to smile but was still in shock with what was happening around me.

Frank held out his hand and I took it, as my dad kissed me on the cheek. "Love you" he said "Love you to dad" before he walked away.

I looked at Frank and then turned to look at everyone else around me and how happy they all seemed to be, some already crying and some giving me a wink and a smile. I look over to my mom and dad as they hold each other for comfort, mom with a tissue in hand. I smile at the friends that I met recently and give Rebecca and Julian that look to say "I'll deal with you later" and glance back to Frank.

I looked at Frank, tanned and as sexy as ever and saw that smile he had been carrying around with him for a while, and now I know why, Frank was about to make me his wife.

I'd know this man for over three years, but fell in love with him in under six months, a man who never gave up to get me, and how I never gave up so that he could have me; it was a price I would pay all over again.

My life went from the ultimate betrayal, kidnapping and more, to my now happy ever after.

The vicar asked if we were all ready to begin, then started to say "We are gathered here today"......

The last words I remembered saying to Frank was "I do."

I glanced over and admired how beautiful Autum looked, I couldn't help but repeat those special words, "for better for worse, for richer for poorer, in sickness and in health, *till death do us part*" a dark evil smile glided across Jacks face as he took one last look at Autum and said "I promise you," this is just the beginning, then left the hotel and headed back towards the airport…

Lightning Source UK Ltd.
Milton Keynes UK
UKOW04f1153031013

218410UK00001B/16/P